VIBRATIONS IN TIME

VIBRATIONS IN TIME

DAVID WATMOUGH

 MOSAIC PRESS
OAKVILLE NEW YORK LONDON

CANADIAN CATALOGUING IN PUBLICATION DATA
Watmough, David, 1926-
  Vibrations in time

ISBN 0-88962-340-6 (bound). - ISBN 0-88962-339-2 (pbk.)

I. Title.

PS8595.A75V52 1986   C813'.54   C86-094392-5
PR9199.3.W37V52 1986

Published by Mosaic Press, P.O. Box 1032, Oakville, Ontario,
L6J 5E9, Canada. Offices and warehouse at 1252 Speers Road,
Unit 10, Oakville, Ontario, L6L 5N9, Canada.

Published with the assistance of the Canada Council and the
Ontario Arts Council.

Design by First Edition Book Creations
Typeset by Speed River Graphics
Printed and bound in Canada

ISBN 0-88962-340-6 cloth
ISBN 0-88962-339-2 paper

MOSAIC PRESS:
In the United States: Riverrun Press Inc., 1170 Broadway, Suite
804, New York, N.Y. 10001, U.S.A.
In the U.K.: John Calder (Publishers) Ltd., 18 Brewer Street,
London, W1R 4AS, England.

DEDICATION

For Floyd and thirty-five years since the roofs of Paris and the rain of Senlis. And also for Charlotte alias Betty, the friend who still teaches me.

Born August, 1926, in London of Cornish stock, David Watmough was educated at The Coopers' Company School and King's College, University of London. After graduation he moved to France where he produced his first work of non-fiction, *A Church Renascent*, which centred on the priest-worker movement and its ecumenical implications.

After living in New York and San Francisco (with a short return in the mid 1950s to London where he worked briefly as a producer for the BBC's famous Third Program) he returned to California as a feature writer for the San Francisco *Examiner*. In 1960 he moved up the coast to Vancouver where he has been based ever since.

A Canadian citizen since 1969 he has lived in the Kitsilano district of his adopted city for the past twenty-five years.

A book of plays, all his fiction, and *The Unlikely Pioneer*, a book devoted to opera in western Canada and tied to the career of Irving Guttman (also published by Mosaic) have all been written in the westcoast city.

Vibrations in Time is the sixth successive volume in the ongoing collection of novels and connected fictions covering the life and times of Watmough's protagonist, Davey Bryant. It is his eleventh book.

VIBRATIONS IN TIME

In the selection of these further chronicles of Davey Bryant I have been guided by that peculiar pendulum effect which is contained within the word vibration, and which we perceive most vividly when undergoing the kind of informing experience which occurs intermittently throughout the stages of our development and decline. Perhaps, initially, we tend to dismiss the phenomenon as mere repetition — forgetting that the very flux of existence and our perpetual changing prohibits truly repeated experience. The two basic certainties, those of birth and death, are paradoxically, as novel as they are familiar whenever we observe them. For our insights change as inevitably as our physical seeing throughout our accumulation of years. Nevertheless we bring the resource of memory to each newborn infant beheld or funeral attended. In the juxtaposition of these stories that follow I have striven to so strike chords of memory that Davey's experiences, however singular in themselves, however locked into the specifics of place and private history, can liberate those 'vibrations in time' which can thus be communicated and shared between author and reader. Given the constituents of Davey's life and personality, this is perhaps not an easy task. But for me it is the most meaningful one, and it is in the strength of these universal vibrations that I dare to seek its accomplishment.

David Watmough

CONTENTS

1

THE WOUNDED CHRISTMAS CHOIRBOY

The week that my little Cousin Terence joined our parish church choir
was the time that Uncle Bill's dog, Skip, got caught in the grasscutter up
to Tretawn Farm, and had to have his leg amputated. It was also the
week that Uncle Jan, Mother's older brother, retired from the
blacksmith's forge he had worked for all those years and his son, Wilfrid,
came back from St. German's and took the smithy over.

But what makes me remember that last week in June, 1943 in Cornwall
so precisely wasn't really to do with the blacksmith's shop in St. Tudy to
which I rode our farm horses for shoeing all year round; nor was it the
image of that marvellous rabbiter, Skip, now reduced to one back leg
when digging out a rabbit or rat in the hedge; but the unpleasant feel of
my nose out of joint at Sunday Mass or Evensong when the old hags of our
parish nudged each other and muttered over the new presence of Terence
— and ignored me.

In choirboy terms Master Terence Menhenniot was indubitably a pin-
up job. I had been what in our village of St. Keverne, the elders
grudgingly conceded as "a 'andsome little bugger" as I had first set out
down the Norman aisle in cotta and cassock at the age of ten. But
Terence's looks were of a wholly different order.

Setting aside such ancillary factors as my being now thirteen, at the
end of my chorister's tether, as it were, and with a couple of pimples to
declare with my breaking voice that my ethereal days as a soprano were
rapidly on the wane, eight-year old Terence with his golden curls, had
instantly turned our bevy of worshippers who were invariably inspired by
malice towards mankind in general, and hatred of our High Church
Vicar in particular, into besotted fans.

I suppose the situation was inevitable. For the past three years our
twenty-member choir had found it progressively difficult to sustain its
dozen boys and what new faces Father Trewin had managed to dragoon
into service had proved no competition for me. With their ruddy faces,
straight hair, oafish manners and squawking voices it was perfectly clear
that our parish priest lay more emphasis on the presence of an adequate
number of small boys in starched surplices and black cassocks, than in
their vocal support of the six farmers, the sexton and the schoolmaster
who provided the tenor and bass contributions to our assembly.

But in the Norman church tower, that strange place with the furry
ends of the bell-ropes looped like caterpillars over our heads, and the
broad slate flagstones of the floor littered with owl and bat droppings, I
glumly watched Terence Menhenniot prepare for his debut in the
procession to the choirstalls at the far end of the church, with all the self-
conscious diligence of a Duse or Bernhardt. And in his poise and
confidence as he arranged his cotta over the cassock, and fitted the ruff at

11

his neck — all articles of ecclesiastical apparel which I knew he had never worn before in his life — I recognized both a consummate competitor for the eye of the congregation and a winner to boot.

And so it was. Mrs. Trebilcock, whose whisper was as loud as her reputation for venom was extensive, spoke across the aisle to Mrs. Harry Hoskyns — right after the first two pairs of little boys had passed her pew. "My, that Terence is a proper treat you! 'Tis lovely to have a chile as fetchin' as that one — specially after they other buggers."

I had no doubt, of course, as to the identity of 'they other buggers'. Only the previous Sunday I had overheard her in the church porch, telling Mr. Nankivell who farmed the Glebe, how stuck up all we Bryants were, and how boys like Rob Pengelly, Tom Purdue, Will Carthew and me, with our reputations, shouldn't be allowed in the choir at all. "Sex fiends, they be, Mr. Nankivell. A disgrace to St. Keverne if ever there was!" and her thin mouth had slammed shut with the same moist slap mother made when putting up pounds of fresh butter on the cold slate shelves of the dairy.

I knew the old cow was referring to an unpleasant incident involving twelve year old Molly, Police Constable Apse's daughter, who in a fit of remorse had admitted to mutual anatomical exploration with us four boys on top of Mr. Prouse's freshly made haystack. The woman's vicious attack had concluded by her remarking to Mr. Nankivell that we should be all sent packing from St. Keverne parish church — "'cos they'm really nothin' but a pack of Methodies." The latter being an allusion to the fact that my Aunt Marjorie, after having told Father Trewin that she could see no reason why her five kids couldn't attend both the church and chapel Sunday School outings, had broken with the custom of most of the families in our hamlet of Churchtown and started joining the folks from up Trelill way, who heard uneducated lay preachers rant in the chapel every Sunday morning, instead of Holy Mass.

Unfortunately, Terence Menhenniot's fanclub didn't end with vile Mrs. Trebilcock and her sycophantic cronies — nor was it stimulated only by such ulterior motives as the Bryant hatred which animated her. Father Trewin, who definitely wasn't one of your child-molesters (like the Parson over Rough Tor way, who was always fiddling with his boy scouts) could be seen from his special stall across from us in choir, positively *simpering* over the beauteous newcomer.

And when it transpired, at the very first practice, that my little cousin couldn't even sing on pitch, let alone carry a tune in his head, Father Trewin simply told him not to worry and that it would all come right later, if he persisted.

Then there were those men in the choir who patently favored him over the likes of Rob, Tom, Will, and me, and never watched him with the suspicion and mistrust which they seemed to think wholly in order for the likes of us who were somewhat older and certainly finer vocalists.

The situation didn't improve as Sundays and Greater Feasts passed with the Church's Calendar and those rare but fiscally profitable occasions such as important weddings or the funerals of local notables, which all warranted the choral forces of the Parish Church of St. Keverne and the Blessed Virgin Mary — to give it its full, if rarely used, title.

Each time would see young Terence faithfully present, his curly locks as gorgeous as ever, his peaches and cream complexion unblemished and those wide grey eyes wed to that kissable cupid's bow, ever raised in dutiful supplication towards the lowered cheek of authority: innocence ever at the ready to repay experience.

In the words of the scriptures which we read and sang *'and the flesh of the child waxed warm'* and like King David (of whom we knew much and with whom *I* liked to identify) young Terence *'was ruddy and beautiful'*. Moreover, Terence did develop his singing abilities as Father Trewin had prophesied, and by the end of his first year in the choir his slightly husky, alto voice, could soar beyond that of any of us, and the sweetness and purity of it was so breathtakingly distinctive that (I invariably noted with a scowl) the congregation would readily start to nudge one another and that Trebilcock creature would immediately start her loud talking again.

I began to detest those days when I knew we would be singing such old favorites of mine — because I'd always been given the solos — as *I Know That My Redeemer Liveth* and *Lead Me Lord* for my voice was but a croak and it was now 'golden boy' who warbled to heaven — with or without the uncertain support of aged Miss Cleve at the organ.

Perhaps sensing that Terence was less than popular with his fellow-choristers, the boy's mother, a thin woman named Muriel, began to attend each service at which her only child now sang. She sat erect in the front pew, from where she could see him most clearly and dreamily eye the love of her life. For Muriel Menhenniot, as my mother had told me once when I was complaining about Terence's smug demeanour, had not borne her son until she was forty-two and she and her railwayman husband had despaired of ever becoming parents. That was the reason, my mother asserted, why Terrence was so initially spoiled at home — although that excuse was later compounded by his mother's conviction that her golden-haired son was so delicate that he had to be shielded from the more basic crudities of village life, such as fraternizing with his co-evals and even sharing the various chores which were the lot of our Cornish childhood, regardless of gender, parental wealth, or individual temperament.

So Terence was escorted twice each Sunday to church, just as he was to choir practice on Wednesday evenings. H didn't go to our village school (run by Mr. Oliver Bray who sang baritone) but to a private one where the children wore cherry-red uniforms and looked silly. And even that was not in Wadebridge, our local town, but north of us in Camelford where he took the National bus each day.

Then again, he *never* helped out at hay-making, corn harvest, or threshing when every youngster in the parish was pressed into service; nor was he ever to be seen collecting kindling for the copper and Monday's clothes-wash, up to Tregilderns cottage behind the fig bush, where the Menhenniots lived. Instead, if you please, he was given special voice lessons with Mrs. Wesley Jago, L.R.C.M., all the way up the coast road to St. Minver, which he attended in a big Austin car hired from Hawkey's of Port Isaac. The extravagance of that was so overwhelming that at least our family openly described it as sinful — even though we weren't Methodists, and thus obsessed with money matters.

I have referred to my cousin's smugness — and indeed, he did seem so complacent, so cheerfully expectant of the world's approbation, that there were times when I would gladly have given away my prize ferret, Sam, just to see Master Terence fall arse over tip in the mound of manure I steadily fed each Saturday morning after mucking out the stables. But I have to admit that, accompanying his conviction that the world loved him, even as it treasured his looks and his voice, was an odd kind of innocence. Then if old bitches like Mrs. Trebilcock, usually acidulous men like Oliver Bray, the baritone who sat behind me in the choir, and, of course, his own adoring parents, all turned into simpering idiots when discussing him or in his company, it was surely no surprise that the kid took an awful lot for granted.

But there my charity runs dry. Age did not improve him. One year after his entry into the choir he scarcely bothered to give us, his choral companions let alone his relatives, the time of day. By his tenth birthday he was not only dictating to a usually dictatorial Father Trewin, what he wanted to sing as solos at each service, but had totally ignored our traditional seating in choir, which was based on seniority, and taken over the stall right opposite the vicar — without asking permission of any of us.

Terence's haughtiness was not confined to his activities in our church. That same summer he refused, via his mother, the regular invitation to my August birthday party, which I shared with my cousin Loveday, whose nativity was but two days from mine, and which most of our young relatives attended in the mowey where tressle tables were always erected for the outdoor feast.

In summary, I hardly feel that I am exaggerating when I say that by the time I had left the boys' section of the choir altogether and had become a mere passenger with the men while waiting to discover whether I was going to end up a baritone or a tenor, Terence Menhenniot, pretty-faced star chorister, was talking (or singing, rather) only to God!

I remember what was virtually my last exchange with The Brat (as my brother Jan and I had succinctly dubbed him). It was a Wednesday night in December: the special choir rehearsal, in fact, for the December 8th Feast of Our Lady — the observance of whose Immaculate Conception had been introduced into our parish by its current incumbent, Father Trewin. I had overheard a recent conversation among some of our parish malcontents who objected to this rather exotic celebration. In church, just by the ancient granite font, and almost under the Great Seal of King Charles II given to those of St. Keverne for rallying to the restoration of the monarchy, I myself echoed their sentiments. "That there Immaculate Conception we'm having is really for Papists, you. 'Tidn'n exactly Church of England stuff, is it?"

But it was immediately obvious that The Brat had been well primed by the Vicar. "The Celtic Church is bravun older that Canterbury. We don't have to listen to they for what we can do and what us can't. After all, Davey, half on our saints they never heard on — including St. Keverne our patron!"

"I 'spose you got some special ole job to sing," put in Harry Purdue, my old friend Tom's younger brother. "That's why you'm a backin' of 'ee. Any ole sow-pig can see that! We b'aint born yesterday Terence Menhenniot. I bide you come only for the anthems and they descants."

"Our father says you b'aint here so much for the candlelight as the *limelight*," contributed a small boy who looked like a Cardew but I wasn't quite sure — now that there were so many of them with the ginger hair and freckles, about the place.

"I don't have to listen to none of 'ee," my cousin reorted hotly. "I'm sitting a choral scholarship if you did but know it. Then I shall be singing down to Truro Cathedral and in the choir school there. Shan't be sorry to shake the dust of this silly ole plaice off me feet, neither!"

And with that, plus a complementary toss of those curls which had turned a darker gold since he had first joined the choir, he sailed off in the direction of the church tower where all our music was untidily stacked and where the mice blithely chewed paper and left between our pages, their pellets of digested pleasure.

The Feast of The Immaculate Conception of the Blessed Virgin Mary was duly celebrated according to the dictates of our parish priest, and went off witout a hitch. How I loathed that fine-chiseled little face as I watched it stare up at the oak barrel-roofing of our church, as the sweet stream of sound spewed forth...

Afterwards, outside in the porch, where the Elizabethan stocks, in their wormholed antiquity, ranged the graite wall and from whose rafters rows of sleepy pipistrelle bats hung, amid a few terse and softspoken disapprovals of the service, I actually heard Muriel Menhenniot sobbing her pleasure at the transporting joy her son's voice had just afforded her. And that Terence nearly having to be immaculately conceived himself! I wanted to vomit instead.

But fortunately I didn't and my iron self-control was very soon rewarded. We had no sooner gotten over the Immaculate Conception when we had to turn our attention to the Christmas festivities. Now that particular year what we call in our family, our 'English cousins' were coming down from London to escape the Labor Government and the postwar shortages. It was what they called 'Austerity' up there and my mother felt that her sister and family would benefit from a bit of Cornish

15

cooking and all the fresh farm and dairy produce that were available to us, as well as a few of the early vegetables from Penzance and The Scillies that would have cost the earth up to London.

Apart from the minor upheaval of stretching the resources of Polengarrow farm to contain ten people instead of the normal five, it also meant that my first cousin, Arthur, whom I had last seen as a baby, would be arriving. Well, he not only arrived, looking incredibly like a younger version of Terence to whom he was distantly related, but immediately asked whether he would be able to sing in our choir on Christmas morning, as he would have done in Wimbledon church had he stayed at home.

Although I wasn't minded to like small boys, let alone aid their requests, in this case I acted without hesitation. "I do know for a fact that we'm shorthanded down there," I told Arthur, "so I'll slip right down to the Vicarage on me bike and ask Father Trewin if he'll have on 'ee."

Just as I expected, there was no prevarication from that quarter. In fact not only the Vicar, but everyone else with whom I spoke during those days leading up to the holidays, seem strangely elated at the prospect of young Arthur's presence in the chancel of St. Keverne Church. Unusual in that our villagers were disinclined to welcome strangers — even the kin of those who had lived among them for centuries, as had we Bryants.

At Christmastide in St. Keverne's Church that year we went full out. The rood screen was garlanded not only with the traditional evergreens, the holly and the ivy, but we even managed to scour the protected hedgerows and dells of the immediate countryside to yield a few early primroses and we also had some hardy roses from Uncle Joe Yelland's cottage with its secluded southern aspect, plus some usual winter jasmine from our farmhouse garden. The latter made a rich yellow frieze about the font and behind the altar of the Lady Chapel.

In 1947, I recall, we still had only candles and oil lamps for illumination as my Great Uncle Herbert didn't provide electricity (in memory of his wife) until the following year. But what with the sumptuous musical setting for Midnight Mass and the decorative efforts extending over three days by the women of the parish, even little Arthur, with all his London sophistication, was entranced with what he saw when the two of us entered the church the afternoon of Christmas Eve. We were there because our young visitor had asked if he might have a prior look at the music as he had been unable to attend earlier choir practices — a professional attention to detail, I duly noted, that far exceeded anything that Terence had ever demonstrated.

All my hopeful anticipations over Arthur were realized from the very moment the solemn procession of Christmas including the blessing of the crib, wound us up and down the shadowy aisles to the words and tune of the hymn, *Adeste Fideles*. Not only did his animated face, bathed in the soft glow of oil lamps, yield an innocence and piety which made the overly familiar Terence look positively corrupt, but Wimbledon's soprano quite blotted out in range and sweetness, the efforts of Master Menhenniot. And if it was thus in the opening hymn, it was ever more so as the Liturgy unfolded. By the time we reached the Plainsong Setting of that lovely phrase from the Gradual: *"the dew of thy birth is of the womb of the morning"*, Terence had succumbed to the sulks and was silent while the rest of the boys gladly followed suit to allow the full force of Arthur's mastery of Gregorian chant, and ethereality of tone, to fill first the candle-bright choirstalls and sanctuary and then the great length of the nave itself. I looked quickly in the direction of Father Trewin, hoping that the priest was at least acknowledging that a greater than Terence had come among us and was gratified to observe the old man's eyes opening and closing in ecstasy. Leering by now in triumph, I turned to feast on the expressions of my fellow-choirmen: white heads and bald ones nodded in grave appreciation of the newcomer in our midst.

Nor was Arthur's devastating effect confined to those of us on the altar side of the rood screen. Out in the packed congregation, Cornish souls melted in the flow of such vocal beauty as my cousin from across the Tamar so felicitously bestowed. In the soft candlelight of the sanctuary Arthur Ingram's features held the delicacy of a Michelangelo sculpture as he soared in descant after descant and solo'd the Plainsong when the older music of the Church usurped the more recent hymns.

Mrs. Trebilcock was seen to take a handkerchief from her large handbag and sob noisily into it and towards the end of the Eucharist — when the Wimbledon nightingale transported us finally on that wondrous and memorable night with the verses of *Once in Royal David's City* soaked in his own special purity — history in St. Keverne parish was made when from isolated spots in the congregation, came the sound of enthusiastic clapping.

Wholly unnerved by the applause, a horrified Vicar gulped his blessing from the altar and Miss Cleve, in panic, (transmitted no doubt by her parish priest) laid too many digits upon the console, causing the organ to sound briefly like a ship's klaxon in a dense fog. The rest, I confess, was anti-climax.

Young Terence, bud-mouth clamped tight, fairly bolted his exit in the final procession down the church to the belltower where we were routinely prayed over and dismissed. But that early Christmas morn Terence didn't linger longer than to yank off his cotta and tear at the multiple buttons of his cassock — as if the garment, too, were an offence not to be borne. Even as Father Trewin muttered a final Hail Mary, our erstwhile star of the choirstalls was pushing open the heavy oak door; tear-glistening eyes in a head held defiantly high.

I did not know then, of course, but he was never to sing in our choir again. In fact that was but the least of it for our toppled alto. For the next several days I put him quite out of mind as young Arthur and his relatives were our preoccupation. But after the Ingrams had left and the wintry rhythms of January had taken over, it gradually became apparent that not only was Terry now missing from choir-practises and the Sunday services, but he was no longer to be seen anywhere in the village. I mentioned this to Mother who in turn informed me that when Father Trewin visited the Menhenniots to enquire after Terence, he was refused entry at Tregilderns cottage by the boy himself who began to scream and shout until the old priest turned sadly away.

I am sure that I would have thought a good deal less about Cousin Terence, now that he was no longer visible, had it not been for a distressing occurrence that March when his father met with a terrible accident at the entrance to the railway tunnel, just south of Port Isaac Road station. Severely mangled as a result of falling between the cars of a freight train, he was taken by ambulance to Tehiddy hospital where he survived for only three days. At the funeral down to St. Keverne, it was noted with shock and incredulity that a sobbing widow was unaccompanied by a mourning son. Muriel Menhenniot, almost hysterical in grief, relied on the succouring ministrations of old Mrs. Trethewey, her next door neighbor, and it was she who led the distraught woman out of the church before the Requiem was concluded.

After that there were many who presented themselves at the cottage behind the fig bush and fuchsia hedge to offer the two remaining Menhenniots their services. But none crossed the threshhold. Either the black-clad Muriel or a progressively dissheveled Terence refused the world entry and shouted and screamed until obeyed. Eventually they were left alone. I recall talk of the district nurse visiting and even mention of a psychiatrist. But that is all rather vague by now. Certainly I never set eyes on Terence again during the remainder of his childhood and youth.

Whether the result of his savage fall from a stellar role in the choir, or the tragedy of his father's premature death, one can only speculate, but the fact remains that the Christmas of 1947 was virtually the last that Terence Menhenniot was seen beyond the confines of Tregilderns and its leafy garden.

It was in 1967 that Mother wrote to me in Vancouver, where I had settled some years earlier, and informed me that Muriel had recently passed on — Mother's letters were little more than St. Keverne obituary lists by this time — and that the stout, balding man who had stood alone as Chief Mourner at her burial service was none other than Terence. Immediately after the commital in the upper graveyard (where she lay flanked by her husband, Fred, and my second cousin Lewis) he left without exchanging a word with anyone save Ned Carhart, the stone mason, about a tombstone — presumably back to Tregilderns and its quiet behind that enormous fig bush.

One other snippet Mother added to her airletter. Terence was now a practised ham radio operator and, according to village gossip, often stayed up all night talking via his microphone to people all over the world.

18

2

THE WAY IT WAS

A Scotsman put me onto a Welshborn Irishman from Cardiff and he gave me a job in the library of Stanford University in California — that was the way the British connection went. At least, that is how this particular Cornishman secured his first pay check as an immigrant in the U.S. of A. back in 1953.

To say I was happy would have been a niggardly description of my emotional state. I was living in California, re-united with my lover, the possessor of a job which centered on books and was full of the energy and optimism of a young man in his early twenties. Bliss! . True, my lover had recently been drafted into the army but he was stationed at nearby Fort Ord and as he was a recent French graduate, we both assumed he would end up in some congenial post such as with the Army Language School in Monterey which was also relatively close at hand.

When I first saw Ken, eight weeks after his induction, he was already a transformed person. I was sitting eating my lunch sandwich at the picnic tables outside the campus snackbar when I heard his voice and quickly turned to confront that face I had first seen some eighteen months earlier in Paris where we had both been students.

It was a sun-dazzled day and as I stared up at him I found it hard to make his features out. But it wasn't only the glare from on high in the February blue creating the difficulty. The U.S. Army had changed more than his clothes, divested him of more than a sweater, T-shirt and khaki chinos. I was squinting up at the most handsome man I had ever known! When we had met in that room full of grad students on the rue Auguste Vacquerie in the posh Paris of the 16e arrondissement, I had immediately thought Ken attractive. His lively mind — far more informed and disciplined than mine — his boyish enthusiasm, his American 'innocence', were things which although I didn't envy, I at once longed to share.

Of course I couldn't have his six foot three inches, his blue eyes and — to a European — an intriguingly different gait — but within hours of meeting him I was visiting the official U.S. Library on the Champs Elysees and soaking up 'his' culture with such books as Sherwood Anderson's *Winesburg, Ohio,* and striving to absorb the country which had birthed and shaped him via a fat, journalistic volume by John Gunther, entitled *Inside USA.*

But that was September, 1951 and that was Ken Bradley, student at the Sorbonne, recent Stanford graduate and even more recently, brought out as gay on the *S. S. Flandre* by a suave young Protestant pastor whom I had hated at first mention. And this was 1953 and the muscle-shaped adonis blocking me from the harsh rays of the sun, with a body turned golden-brown by the open rifle range and bush country of Fort Ord army

19

base, was Private Ken Bradley — in training to help conclude the U.N. Operation in Korea. I had fallen instantly in love with a handsome student but I was now rejoined by a young Californian male whose beauty, freshly sculpted by the military, made me want to swoon....

"Hi, Davey. Recognise me?" my lover asked with a grin. "I just hitch-hiked back to campus. Where're you staying?"

I was still delightedly devouring the transformation when his words impinged and I was suddenly afraid. That is to say I felt cold cramps in my belly and my mind churned with anxiety over where I was staying and whether it would be possible for Ken to stay there with me.

When he'd left for the army I had had a room in the Deke House (arranged by Ken with a friend of his who acted as a kind of manager for the fraternity) but just three days earlier I'd left there when my boss at the library suddenly offered to rent me a room in his spacious house beyond the university golf course.

Liam O'Malley had been something of a fairy godfather since my arrival on campus — ostensibly to take post-graduate courses in Creative Writing but in reality to join Ken after our nine months' separation when his French government scholarship had run out and I had to save money by giving English lessons to Parisians to pay my fare and follow him all the way across an ocean and a continent to his natal state.

There had been first the job, albeit a lowly one returning books to the library stacks but still wage-paying work entitling me to a social security number, and then the offer of a room in his house — I surely did have every reason for gratitude to Liam O'Malley. Nor had the benisons stopped there. Each night since I had moved in he plied me with Bushmill's Irish whiskey (which he himself liberally imbibed) and then talked knowledgeably of novels and authors he felt I should know. It was enthralling talk and I had a real sense of learning from this erudite Irishman with the dense black crew-cut and stolid girth which he wedged into his favorite armchair as he poured out both the amber liquid and the sense of his extensive learning.

Yet he was scant of small talk and his puffy face with its rather small eyes devoid of much expression contrived to put me somewhat in awe of him. It was this sense of awe which surfaced now as I visualized Ken moving in with me for his very first weekend of leave. Liam had talked uninhibitedly of his life as an officer in the British army during the Burma campaign. He used cuss-words liberally and was not squeamish in his details of dysentery or the general human response to pain and wounding. But even as I had listened to his racy anecdotes, dutifully laughing at his quips and frowning at his vividly evoked horrors, I experienced a sense of nervous reservation. It was a subtle thing, hard to pinpoint, but it was tough enough, persistent enough, to return now as Ken informed me his things were at the main library desk and that he hoped he could bed down in my rented room in the O'Malley residence.

Liam O'Malley was a committed Catholic and although he was

constantly making ribald remarks about the Hierarchy and even rude jokes tainted with blasphemy (at least to my decorous Anglican tastes) about confessionals and parish priests, he rarely failed to attend Mass each Sunday, he informed me, and he particularly favored the Catholic novels of such a minor writer as Bruce Marshall as well as the 'biggies' such as Graham Greene, Evelyn Waugh and the Frenchman, Francois Mauriac.

"I think it will be all right," I said cautiously, as we walked amid reclining bodies that lunchtime, towards the library steps. "He's a bit of an oddball but I don't think he'll object." Then I had a brainwave and my expression brightened accordingly. "I know! Let's tell him, Ken, that you're my American cousin. We'll say your Dad is my mother's brother. You can tell him —"

"Why?" (If my face had lightened my companion's had abruptly clouded.) "Why pretend anything? You're not ashamed of me, are you Davey?"

"Of course not." I might have added that I was a little afraid of Liam O'Malley, but I couldn't bring myself to admit that to Ken. "It would be just that much more easy to explain things that way." I told him. But I was nevertheless glad that he didn't press the subject further.

We found Liam in his office to the left of the enquiry desk. He could not have been more affable, rising as we entered, smiling broadly at us in turn. Even so, my caution did not go away. "This is my second-cousin, Ken Bradley," I compromised. "His father and my mother are cousins. We have the same great-grandmother in Cornwall."

Liam grinned yet more expansively. "That indeed would follow if you were second cousins," he observed. "Haven't I seen you before?" he asked Ken. "I'm a Stanford graduate and was back doing grad work when I got drafted," Ken explained.

"That's right. I've seen you in the stacks. Let me see, you were in arts. Languages, wasn't it?"

I mentally cursed the librarian for his accurate memory and was thankful for my brainwave about second cousinship.

"French was my major, Spanish my minor," Ken told him. "But I'm really interested in literature, period. Davey tells me he thinks you've forgotten more fiction that he'll ever know."

Liam's small eyes widened in pleasure. "I suppose I have read quite a bit. Then there was ample opportunity for a book-hungry young subaltern when I was in Egypt and the desert. Right up to when I joined Wingate and his bloody Chindits in Burma. From then on I spent my time looking for Japs — not reading pages of print!"

"You make my soldiering sound very tame!" Ken told him, laughing. "The only enemy we have to watch out for are rattlers."

"Still, Boyo — armies are armies. If you end up in Korea you'll soon learn what I mean."

This was not a conversation I found at all congenial. "Ken has only a

21

48 hour pass and nowhere to stay. It's too far for him to visit his parents," I added. "Would it be all right if he shared my room, Mr. O'Malley? I'll pay the extra rent if it's o.k. with you and Mrs. O'Malley."

The librarian came round from his desk, stood between us and put his arms around both our shoulders." Of course you can stay, young Bradley. Allow an old captain of Her Majesty's Irish Yeomanry to extend his hospitality to an infantryman of the United States Army. Who knows, it might expedite my citizenship. I've applied for my first papers, you know."

I was so relieved that Ken was to have a roof for the next two nights and so excited by the prospect of our sharing a mattress after all the weeks of our separation that I turned to our portly benefactor. "O thank you so much! You're an absolute angel!" But even as the words spurted out I sensed their campy extravagance. "Our two mothers will be so pleased to hear of your kindness," I added quickly.

"Come to dinner," O'Malley invited. "Marguerite and I will be delighted to entertain you on your first leave."

I listened to Ken's ready acceptance and was impressed by even more than his recent demonstration of tact and diplomacy. The army had apparently changed so much more than his physical looks. Talking now to O'Malley he seemed much more confident and assured than when I'd seen him off on the Greyhound to Monterey that dismal Saturday morning.

We left the librarian and walked through the Inner Quad. "You sure struck it lucky with old O'Malley," Ken said cheerfully. "God, it would have been marvellous enough if he'd just provided us with a bed where I could really say hello to you. But we're in for a slap-up meal as well! You know, Davey, since I've been in this outfit I'm starving all the time. And not just for food but for you, too!"

I thrilled to his admission for Ken rarely talked that way. But I was still hesitant about my new landlord. "We must be careful," I warned. "I don't think his wife likes me, Ken. And — well, did you notice the funny look he gave me when I thanked him?"

"You worry too much. You're getting paranoid in your old age. Don't forget what you told me when you took me to Cornwall to meet your parents. 'All the world loves a lover' you said — and it worked, didn't it? Not only with your Mom and Dad and your brothers. But with Aunt Martha and Cousin Jan, too. So why not now with the O'Malleys? Answer me that."

I looked at him. The trouble was I couldn't. I had no cogent answer to his reasoning. All I wanted to do was to reach up on my toes and clasp the six-foot three of him and cover that sun-tanned face with kisses. "It'll be all right," I agreed. But I spoke as much in hope as conviction.

The supper with the O'Malleys came off better than I'd anticipated. True, Marguerite made only fleeting appearances as she seemed much occupied in the kitchen and with those of her brood who had been delegated by Liam as paterfamilias, to help her. There were five children: four boys and a girl. However, Mrs. O'Malley was heavy with a sixth child. All of the youngsters, whose ages extended from one to seven, had empathically Celtic names — from the scion, Liam, Jr. and his sister Colleen, through Patrick and Brendan to little Sean. They were pasty kids, forever wailing and comically ugly. The ears of the boys rose to almost a point, making them look like leprechauns. Their father largely ignored them, only yelling and striking out when their commotion disturbed his discourse. This didn't happen during supper when I thought them uncharacteristically silent, giving Ken an endless series of side-glances and hiding in groups behind the grease-stained skirt of their tall and scrawny mother on the rare times she stood there in the dining room with us.

Shortly after we had consumed a strong-smelling stew and the tart plums and lumpy castard which followed it, Marguerite and her young returned permanently to the kitchen and Liam invited us into the book-lined living room which led directly in from the front door. It was a large and rambling house of ill-design and rendered untidy not only from the efforts of five undisciplined children but Liam's habit of taking various books from shelves and leaving them on the much-worn beige carpet about his armchair.

It had occurred to me before Ken's arrival that perhaps the Irishman subconsciously expected library assistants to return such volumes to his personal 'stacks', but instead the discarded books merely collected dust and grew higher and higher from the floor — where they perched precariously until falling from Pisa towers of three and four feet.

Other than the presence of Ken the remainder of that evening addressed very much the same contours as on those occasions when Liam and I sat there sipping Irish whiskey and talking books.

I recall some discussion of a book about the British army in Malaya called *Look Down in Mercy* by a Walter Baxter, which Liam extolled extravagantly. But by then he was markedly in his cups and when I stole a glance at my lover it was to note that he, too, bore a flush quite unconnected with the suntan I had noticed when he had first greeted me that noon.

When Liam's puffy eyes were near to being closed I nudged Ken and suggested that after all his strenuous training he must be ready to crash. He at once caught my drift and an erotic current passed between us. In seconds we had risen and made our goodnights to a rather disconcerted host — it was only one o'clock and thus early for him — and fled upstairs towards the mutually longed-for bed.

How describe that first night of reunion for our youthful, lust-hard bodies? Over subsequent years I have told myself it was the most satisfying sexual experience I have ever known. And if only Ken and I ever spoke about such things, I am sure he would say the same. We did not spend many minutes asleep on that February night in the house nestled amid the foothills, west of Palo Alto. Once or twice we bumped against the partition wall in our endless writhings and there was some moment in the torrid wastes of the small hours when I thought I detected an answering thump from the adjacent bedroom where the O'Malleys slept. I at once fell still and held Ken tight. But soon the kindled pleasure was once more not to be denied, and our frantic coupling broke out again.

Next morning, when O'Malley drove us back on campus, my landlord seemed his normal, taciturn self — laconic but even amiable. I happily concluded that our strenuous love-making had not disturbed his drunken sleep. My small apprehensions rolled away well before we hungrily tackled breakfast at a diner we knew, along the El Camino, which we walked to down the long length of Palm Drive leading off the campus.

Still buoyant with youthful energy we then retraced our steps and spent the rest of the morning listening to cicadas on the grassy knoll behind the Music Building of Lagunita, occasionally aware of buck-teethed gophers poking up sleek heads from the safety of their burrows, even as we dimly felt the presence of several students sprawled about the sun-warmed turf. But none of it really impinged. I could think only of the previous night and the one which was to come. By lunchtime our bodily feelings were making us so restive that when Ken suggested a visit to the library where he wished to examine various French periodicals he'd missed at Fort Ord, I readily concurred.

When he was sitting behind a pile of journals in the Periodicals Room I sauntered over to the general catalog where, on whim, I looked up the book which Liam had praised so fulsomely before the two of us. I was amazed, not to say perturbed, on examining the one copy in the stacks, to find that *Look Down in Mercy* was a novel about men and that it didn't shie away from delineating homoerotic relationships. Yet that important fact had not been brought up by my boss and host. Within his paeans of praise for the book he had referred to army life and jungle circumstances in its pages — but not a word pertaining to gay life or love had passed his lips. To be sure the year was 1953 when covert attitudes to such matters still emphatically reigned, but this was also The Returned Warrior and Prodigious Reader, Liam O'Malley — and his particular silence on the subject in our presence now disturbed me. I put the volume back on its metal shelf and returned to my lover, heavy with thoughts.

Ken looked up at me a little surprised. We had agreed to spend the bulk of the afternoon there in the library, hoping to eventually cadge a lift back to the house when Liam quit for the day. But it was quite obvious from my demeanour that I wanted to vacate the place at once. In fact I blurted out as much as he gathered up his few possessions, his forage cap and a couple of sheets of paper on which he had obviously (and from what I suspected of army life, needlessly) been taking notes from articles he'd discovered in the *Mercure de France* and *Le Figaro Littéraire*. "If we go straight back to the O'Malley place those awful kids will be milling around everywhere and that could be very frustrating for us." I grinned, seeing immediately the track his mind was taking. "Let's not go back there then. Let's go for a long walk in the hills. I've never been up there. No one walks around here, you know."

Normally Ken would have taken up the cudgels right away in defense of the mores in his native state. But not this time. Perhaps the army had made him less prickly to my European taunts — or perhaps I looked sufficiently worried for him to let it ride. In any case, we hadn't gotten as far as Lasuen Boulevard before he started to interrogate me. "What's the matter now, my dear? You see a ghost back in the stacks? Did fat O'Malley put the make on you when you were kneeling for a book?"

"Just that novel he was going on about last night. After dinner? Guess what the subject's all about?"

Ken gestured vaguely as we walked. "The British in Burma or Malaya, wasn't it? World War Two and all that?"

"It's about two men in love. It's as much *that* kind of book as *Finistère* or *Strange Brothers*," I said referring to two fairly recent gay novels we had both read in Paris.

"Perhaps your Mr. O'Malley is trying to tell us something," Ken suggested.

"Are you kidding? With five kids and another little bastard on the way?"

"Maybe he's surfeited in that direction. Poor old Marguerite looks like a scarecrow. I reckon he's shagged her into nothing! Apart from that baby bulge she's all bone. I'm sure she rattles when they're going at it," he added. Ken prodded me gently in the middle of the spine. "You're not that silent yourself, come to that. Anyway, let's talk about other things than the O'Malleys. I've only got one more day and I want to concentrate on us."

I smirked. "Yeah — and it isn't just talk you want, you filthy, sex-starved swine!"

"I'm in better shape than you," Ken retorted. "Come on, I'll race you to the turn-off for the barn."

It was then I recalled the running races of the past. Not so much since I had arrived in America but first in Paris (in the Bois or down the Avenue Foch leading to it) and then on the Cornish moors near my parents' farm. I had invariably beaten him for short laps — then his longer legs would win out. "Only up to the eucalyptus trees," I shouted. But this time I couldn't pass him, couldn't even keep pace with him although I gave it all I got.

When we arrived at the grove of clean-smelling gum trees where the land opened out in green and gently undulating slopes, I was gasping for breath but full of joy. Ken had run like a deer — all the gangly ungainliness of the past now abandoned. Once more I was keenly proud of what the army had done for my lover.

We lay self-consciously, romantically, idyllically under the cloudless sky and watched tiny blue butterflies dance about the slightly sereing grass of the hillside. From an invisible pond frogs croaked and high up in the lofty blue, larks hovered and piercingly sang. I softly remarked that I loved Ken more than ever and that the magic moment, there on the green clad slope, would never die as a memory, however long I lived. He countered by informing me that he had been steeled through every drill in broiling heat, every gruelling small arms practice, every exhausting assault course, and all the mindless barracks discipline, by the prospect of this weekend reunion with me. I think that perhaps we were both a little extravagant in our claims, in the rhetoric of proclaimed fidelity and in the inflated descriptions of the aching void bred by our separation. But I certainly know we were happy in that hour, rich in our recollection of the passed night and in our tingling anticipation of that which was to come.

And come, of course, it did. We were both of us so full of the prospect that our meal with the O'Malleys — a stale repeat of the night before — was an empty, choreographic gesture. I could have supped on sawdust sandwiches for all my interest in Marguerite's cuisine, and the subsequent Irish and sodas in conjunction with the protracted, bookish talk was just a miserable impediment to that exploratory moment between the sheets we were both so impatiently waiting for.

If the sexual linking of the previous night had been a heavenly intimation, this second renewal of our erotic binding was an ecstasy that could know no topography — celestial or otherwise. Somehow we fled all human bondage and returned to a liberated state of being that drained us of all puss of guilt and puritan rectitude. We rejoiced in sheer carnality, where flesh worshipped flesh, no books were read, no potions drunk, and no music heard. There was little room for ratiocinative memory and so, naturally, the sole inheritance was an undefined joy: a blurred encapsulation, the aspic of which was broken but once when a sudden, thrusting heave of one against the other led to a violent creaking of bedsprings and a resounding thud against the wall by the side of the bed.

There had been that similar moment on the first night but there was now an extra athleticism, stronger whispers of consummation, and sharper conflicts with inanimate objects. For perhaps I have again exaggerated, perhaps there *was* a serpent of awareness in our fleshly Eden. It was the sense that a Greyhound bus would be taking my lover away from me the following day. Yes, this was surely the thought which lent desperation to our already extravagant efforts at physical union.

We shall never know if the acoustics of our lovemaking during those two marvelllous nights bore a specific price-tag. To the contrary, our only certitude was the richness of shared experience which sustained us through the salt-eyed anguish of leave-taking at the Palo Alto bus depot. I stood huddled and forlorn, not knowing when, if ever, I would see Ken again. For I knew — however much I tried to repress the fact — that armies sent musicians to cookhouses, made killers out of dreamers, and that French-speaking Private Bradley might easily be sent to the combat zone of Korea, the place which had necessitated his uniform in the first place.

O'Malley had driven us into town. He stood apart as we enacted our farewells. Eyes met and hung in soft glances, but Ken's warm breath remained remote from my face. And the permitted handshake was a blasphemy of what we felt and what our arms strained to do as we submitted to the dictates of the straight world as to what constituted a leitimate goodbye between grown men: a soldier and a civilian...

Not surprisingly, as I drove back as passenger in O'Malley's Mercury, I sought silence. But my boss exhibited what I could only consider a perverse bout of loquacity. He wouldn't stop talking and much of his stupid noise was a pestering me with questions.

"You're a close-knit family I gather? My own children aren't like that with their siblings. Have you had time to notice?"

"They're still very young," I said shortly.

"Have you known your cousin — that is, your *second* cousin, for a long time? I mean he was born and raised her in California, wasn't he?"

"They visited us a lot. Especially when my grandmother — I mean my great-grandmother — was still living."

"Really? I should've thought the war and travel restrictions..." he trailed off — but not without bestowing me a heavy look. It spelled "You're a bloody liar." We drove in silence after that.

That night I slept alone in that single bed which had so felicitously made allowances for twin bodies ardently entwined. I was so sad. Not just because I had bidden my lover goodbye that afternoon and didn't know when we would be next together. (He'd hinted at the propriety of visiting his parents when his week's leave came due at the wind-up of his basic training.) But we had no inkling of where he'd be sent after leaving the Fort Ord base. There was only one thing that seemed inevitable in spite of our hopeful references to The Army Language School and Monterey: it would not be at Stanford University where sat a bereft Davey Bryant and his needs!

That melancholy which threatened to engulf me as I lay between those sheets which would not warm was so much more than sorrow for farewell. I grieved over the fact we were not able to say goodbye like other lovers, I grieved over the judgemental presence of Liam O'Malley, and I also grieved over the whole drear plight of being gay and thus so vulnerably in love in a heterosexual world where we were always at *their* beck and call and so much bullied into falsely echoing *their* sentiments and acting in *their* fashion.

Depression took off from there. I wished in the darkness that I wasn't so bloody middle class and thus prey to convention. I remembered those wildly effeminate black boys in Manhattan with peroxided hair and couldn't-care-less gestures with their undulating bodies. And I wished I could be like them. I thought of poorly paid waiters and out-of-work actors who freely called each other 'Mary' and usually opted for female pronouns when describing themselves — and wished I were sufficiently emancipated to do the same.

I am ashamed to say that before sleep took me finally away from all this questing and doubting and spurts of self-pity, I even hankered for freedom from Ken and the clumsy weight of being part of a couple in a world where being single and unencumbeed seemed to make life so much easier.

If you are young enough to think such thoughts on my part now seem ludicrously dated in the 1980s (when even the Stonewall Riots have become gay history) the efficiency of the international mails back there in 1953 must seem mediaeval to you! It was only ten days after Ken's departure that I received the following letter. It bore a Swiss stamp and had a Geneva postmark:

Dear Davey Bryant:

I have heard from my friend Leslie Hertford of Stanford University who writes expressing some worry about you and your current life in California. You may recall first meeting me in London and then again in Paris. The first of our encounters was in your Michaelmas Term at King's College in 1949 and then at a World Council of Churches' Committee meeting in Paris the following year. Indeed, I gather you mentioned the fact to Leslie who thus felt that perhaps I was the best person for him to write and express his concern about what he had heard from a faculty colleague, Liam O'Malley. It would seem that the friends you have made at Stanford, more particularly your *Christian* friends, are anxious about some of the dubious company in which you have been seen. I am sure that you will be immediately able to allay fears in this context. But you will readily understand why a concerned and loving Methodist Pastor such as Leslie Hertford would write to me, an Anglican Bishop, about a young man who claims my acquaintance and whom in fact I had always regarded highly as a student, first at your university and subsequently in Paris where you were richly pursuing your ecumenical enquiry into recent activities of the Church in France. I would certainly appreciate such an assurance from you that all is well and that you are not finding student companionship an occasion of sin. For I could then write to your parents, Father Brand in Paris, and your college Dean — all of whom have been subject, I gather, to some apprehension over your spiritual state — largely owing, I fear, to your protracted epistolary silence.

With the hope, dear Bryant, that this pastoral enquiry, stemming as it does from my keen concern, is possibly unnecessary, I remain as always,

Your Father in God, Trevor Stephens.

I read this communication with its broad letters and detailed flourishes no less than three times. Then I carefully folded it, returned it to its envelope, and finally placed it at the bottom of my travelling trunk which had sailed the Atlantic with me. (Cornish prudence suggested you never knew when a bishop's letter might be valuable — even if the contents pissed you off!)

I had picked up that sole piece of mail at the post office during my lunchtime. Back at the Library I went straight to O'Malley's office to inform him that I would be yielding the room I rented from him just as soon as I could find alternative accommodation. I didn't mention the letter but suggested I needed a place less cut off from social intercourse with campus life. He didn't demur but told me I needn't rush matters on his account. However, he did add that his son, Liam, would take over the room as soon as I'd vacated it as he needed privacy from his brothers and sisters. The librarian then returned his attention to some papers on his desk.

Early the following month when I had moved to the other side of campus, to a basement room on Junipero Serra Boulevard, I received another missive from Bishop Stephens.

11 Rue d'Anjou
Geneva 3e.

My Dear Bryant:

I understand that you have changed your place of residence but I gather you still use the same post office box for your correspondence. Am I to understand from your silence that you are reproving me for unwonted interference in your private affairs? I hope very much hope that is not so. Reverend Hertford tells me he bumped into you at the University and that although you were generally non-committal, he received the distinct impression that you were in receipt of my last letter and felt at variance with my suggestions.

Please try and understand that I wrote (even as I write now) as a Christian who is duty bound to echo St. Paul's admonishments in 1 Corinthians 6:10 over those who will not see the Kingdom of Heaven, even as I am, in all conscience, troubled by what seems to be the state of your spiritual life. It is thus my bounden duty to urge you to stay away from those sins of the flesh we can collate under the heading of perversions and abominations of the Cities of the Plain.

So clearly do I perceive my task in this respect that I am bound 'to speak the truth in love' as the Apostle prescribes, and to advert others of your relationship with this particular young man over whom you have paraded your illicit affection and dramatized your perverse lust within the hallowed confines of a practising Christian home. I am sure you will be hearing from closer friends but not greater enthusiasts for your salvation.

Sorrowfully, T. Stephens

He proved as good as his word. I heard from my parents — my father, that is. I haven't kept the letter but it said something about steering clear of strangers (very Cornish advice, that!). He also sent greetings to Ken and hoped he was having a better time in the U.S. Army than he himself had known in the Imperial Camel Corps during World War One. The postscript — Dad never failed to provide one — told me not to tell details of my private life to Tom, Dick and Harry. For the latter I read bishops, priests and deacons for I knew my father, unlike Mother, had little time for the clergy.

I also heard from Dean Monk. He was blunter than Cornwall or Geneva.

"...You were already displaying a definite lack of contrition over your inverted instincts when here at college, and this further intelligence of your persistent liaison with that fellow-sodomite whom you met in France and thus out of my jurisdiction, only confirms my gloomiest anticipation for your future as a catamite. You are fortunate in taking refuge in a place like California where law and order are of little consequence. Nevertheless, do not be surprised if your police record for importuning and soliciting follows you eventually across the Atlantic. God will not be mocked."

The arrival of that letter sharply modified my resolution to remain mute in face of all this correspondence inspired by that bastard, O'Malley. To Bishop Stephens I wrote succinctly:

"I think you delude yourself. You are not a high-minded prelate brimming with love and compassion but an interfering, gossip-loving bigot whose glib practise of handing out biblical texts to homos like me should be offset by informing all female members of your supposed flock that the misogynist St. Paul informs them that they belong to their husbands (1 Cor. chap.7) and are inferior to them. You can also remind them to read 1 Cor. chap. 14 verses 34-35 where the same old woman-hater insists that women should shut their mouths in public places and if they want to know anything to meekly ask their husbands at home. Get around those idiotic and unfair rules for women if you can!"

Dean Monk got even shorter shrift:

My meeting with my lover two years ago has proved the best thing that has ever happened to me. I strongly advise you to move on from just pawing students, as you did me for four years, to finding a lifetime lover (male) for yourself. You will then grow immeasurably in spiritual power and range of sympathy. See you in paradise — where I am sure you will be dropping beads if you haven't started beforehand!"

In my letter to my parents I made no reference to my private life but said I hoped to see Ken again soon and that his army training was about over. I also asked my Dad if he had a snap of himself on his camel for my scrap-album.

I ignored the Reverend Leslie Hertford when I next saw him approaching although he smiled and called out something in jocular vein. I made sure I was never in a position to have to talk to Liam O'Malley and after speaking with Ken who telephoned me later that week, arranged to leave Stanford altogether and to take the train to Poughkeepsie, New York where I knew a clerical job of sorts had been arranged for me at Vassar College for Women.

Both Ken and I felt rather crushed by these epistolary events and although neither of us admitted it to each other then, just a little scared. Flight for me, we agreed, was the best thing and with his unexpected news of being posted to France, my going to New York State at least meant that we would be a little closer than if I stayed in California. So I went, and that was the end of Liam O'Malley in our lives. Almost, that is...

POST SCRIPTUM

...I saw Ken as he circled the block for the cheaper parking lot, prior to ushering me into the Hudson's Bay Department Store for our annual joint shop. He didn't see me standing there. I was thinking that I must remind him to get a haircut. Those gray locks of his were far too long and straggly. The days of the counter-culture were ten years over at the very least. We'd given up our onkhs and our dried arbutus beads. There was no reason why our heads shouldn't be neat again.

As he got out of the Peugeot and waved in greeting he called out to me. "That lovebird of yours, that cockatiel? There's an egg of the bottom of its cage. You'll have to change its name from Captain Ahab to Stewardess Ahab!"

I laughed, and we embraced there in the Vancouver street before proceeding on to our white-sales shopping expedition. We were just inside the store, which was crowded enough to make me grumpy, when Ken touched my elbow. "Captain-now-Stewardess Ahab made me forget. There was an item in the paper. Remember old O'Malley at Stanford? Well, he retired apparently, from the head librarianship of a college in Ontario. He must have come up to Canada like us. Then his wife was from the prairies, wasn't she? Anyway, when he retired he went to live in Florida where, according to *The Province*, he died yesterday."

Two middle-aged gents of thirty-two years shared life exchanged glances at the shirt counter. Then Ken led a reluctant me toward's men's underwear where I knew he would succeed in stocking me with underpants and T-shirts for the whole year ahead.

3

THE SAVAGE GARDENER

I sat reading by the New Jersey lake; a middle-aged man returned to a metallic sheet of tree-lined water, first known over twenty years earlier, when I was still slim, alcoholically abstemious and full of hope.

Earlier that morning, back in the spacious, architect-designed house of red cedarwood, the talk had been of a son's recent marriage, a daughter's prospective nuptials, and of the possible removal by my two friends, the Polawskis, to farmhouse life in Massachusetts above the Connecticut River, for the next stage of their existence as they attended and finally took on the status of grandparents.

I watched two men fishing from a shallow-draft, metal craft, as I lifted my eyes from the Davis Grubb novel at the sound of water slapping, and the low mutter of their voices. They met my glance, I thought rather coldly. As if I had no right to be sitting on Bill's and Elsa's dock. Then it occurred to me that their hostility — if such it was — may have alternatively been occasioned by my slightly effeminate appearance in that I was wearing a multi-colored shirt with short sleeves which revealed a bangle on my wrist which friends had given me for my fortieth birthday.

A gang of drunken youths had shouted derisively at me back home in Vancouver when walking the dogs along the beach, the previous week. I had been similarly clad and had sported identical jewellery. The memory of that incident was unpleasantly vivid and was frequently recurrent.

I stirred, closed my book, even as the boat with the men drifted by and was finally hid from my sight by the scrim of pale green tracery on the shore-lined trees that bowed low over the water. I got up and stared down from the dock at the brownish depths. It was clear enough, though, to see the mud upon the bottom and an occasional small fish questing through the weeds. I remembered skinny-dipping from that jetty one warm midnight, with Bill and Elsa, God knows how many years before, when with slurred voices and much laughter, we had run with two or three other dinner guests, down the steep slope of the path, impervious to the sharpness of pebbles, to the water's edge — and dived in.

In retrospect it is possible to say that a measure of innocence had prevailed then — though honesty forces me to recall that I had more than a fleeting awareness of the body of another guest, and had indeed done my share in guiding the assembly into its corporate decision to shed garments and plunge into the lake. I was keenly desirous of seeing one, Carlos, a Cuban friend of our host and hostess — in the state that nature had made him.

Nor had I been disappointed. Though quite unaware, I am sure, of the lubricious thoughts concealed behind my open English face, brick-red from sunburn, the young Latin (as is generally the wont with his kind) was prepared to take the tribute of eyefull worship of his smooth and finely curved body, from whatever quarter it originated. I fed, in the moth-fluttering electric light, on the sweat-glistening pectorals, the slim hips and substantial member in its full halo of pubic hair, before watching his tight buttocks disappear below the lake's surface, and quickly followed in pursuit.

As far as the skinny-dipping party and of Carlos and myself, that was that. Sorry, no occasion here for erotic revelation: no chance for fleshly union presented itself that summer's night. In fact I never saw the young man again. Ken and I returned to Canada in a day or so and Elsa told me in a letter, several months later, that Carlos had returned to Havana in those pre-Castro days.

Nevertheless the recollection was a sweet one; easily summoned in pleasurable detail as I stood there that late May morning and deliberated upon that lost opportunity all those years ago, and wondered whether now, so much more *experienced*, so much more *hungry*, so much more *brazen*, I would have handled things differently.

I have always owned the ability to day-dream with sufficient energy to wholly forget the present and to become quite oblivious to my immediate surroundings. It was the case that morning, alone by the man-made lake outside Milltown, New Jersey. I could not only 'see' Carlos' honey-hued torso, his black curls and almost semitically hooked nose, but could likewise 'hear' the shouts, the noisy splashings, and 'breathe' the dank odors of woodland on a humid July night, as well as the oddly earthy smell of the lake water.

I looked up through the tender green leaves, almost expecting the rash of the Milky Way against the black velvet of midnight — instead of the pale blue, and white clouds that this May morning owned. And it was in the sudden shock of celestial recall from such intense reverie, that I became aware of *him*.

A youth, standing there rigidly immobile, some twenty feet away, dressed only in white shorts, tight to his thighs. He was facing the further shore, staring from under dark eyebrows. His hair was black, his skin dusky-gold. He was slim, about nineteen, and his crotch bulged. My mouth was savagely dry but I managed to croak 'Carlos!'

I thought he turned slightly in my direction but he didn't appear to see me. Hungry, horny me! How his youth and beauty stirred the cold of my years — making me long to hold close to that satin flesh to melt the frost of middle-age! In almost one gesture I sucked in my paunch, lifted my greying head to stretch my neck and make my second chin disappear. I thanked God I'd cleaned my teeth and rinsed my mouth that morning, so that stale whiskey, lingering wine fumes, had all been happily banished from my chemically refreshed breath.

"Carlos?" I whispered a second time. "Is it you? In this same place? After all these years?"

Ridiculous questions, of course — deserving of ridiculous answers. But in the heavy spell of such carnal tugging do we make idiots of ourselves.

Only now did he turn in my direction and speak. "Pardon me?"

I could discern no Spanish-accented English, rather the distinct glottal stop of the American east coast. But I was disinclined to linger over such details. I got to my feet, closed my book, and walked towards where he stood in the shade of pin oaks, cherry birch, maples, and tulip poplars that thickly sentinelled the shelving land.

"If your name is Carlos, then I'm meeting my first ghost. But you don't look ghostly with that tan!"

They were surely Carlos' eyes he turned on me at that remark. But unlike twenty years earlier, they seemed remote, distrustful.

"I was looking for Mrs. Polawski," he said. "Like I've finished mowing the lawn out front. She was gonna pay me."

"Mr. and Mrs. Polawski are out and won't be back until around 6 p.m." I told him. "But what if I pay you and then work it out with them?"

He didn't seem too enthusiastic. "Well, I dunno. Like she spoke with me and..."

Realization finally arrived for me. "I'm their houseguest," I explained quickly. "A very old friend visiting from Canada."

He relaxed visibly at that. "I guess I've heard of you. The twins told me you knew their parents. You were all kids together, wasn't it?"

It wasn't, but it was too complicated, I felt, to explain. "Something like that. Now how much is owed you for cutting the lawn?"

I removed my wallet from my hip pocket and took out the wad of green money that Elsa had exchanged at her bank for my multi-colored Canadian bills. The young man came up the steps onto the deck of the dock where I was standing.

"Ten bucks," he said.

I held out a ten dollar bill and as he came closer to take it from my fingers I noticed that he had a small mole at his midriff — just above where faint gold hairs turned darker in their descent beneath his white shorts. For the moment that small expanse of his skin which I meticulously examined, was the most fascinating portion of a human body in the whole, wide world....

I could smell him. Some kind of suntan lotion, I thought, mingling with the sweat released from his exertions with the lawnmower. His own billfold was inserted about the elastic-tuckered waist of his shorts. As he put the money away he spoke up.

"That lawn was a bastard," he informed me. "First time this year, I guess, and that didn't help. But the Polawskis don't have it done regular."

I thought perhaps he was apologizing for the fee he had charged.

"I know what it looked like before you started," I told him. "I don't envy you. And I can tell it was hard work by the sweat on you." I paused briefly. "Lucky you're in such good trim."

Something passed between us. A kind of current. But vague, abstract enough to make it difficult to determine its nature. He glanced at me — and again I was unsure what his expression held: friendliness, or something less pleasant. He next glanced down at the bench table which had the Davis Grubb lying on it. "What you reading?" he asked casually, a rather large hand going out to swivel the title in his direction.

"A novel," I said, adding for no particular reason, "Dr. Polawski lent it to me from his library."

"Yeah. He's got one hell of a lotta books in there. I see 'em when I'm ditching the grass-cuttings. Right up the wall they go. Must be thousands of 'em. Dunno when he's got time to read them all — him being a doctor and that."

He suddenly did a most unconscious, adolescent thing: he eased his equipment within his shorts. Probably his balls were sticky or cramped. I put my hand out to the wooden rail of the dock, where it protruded over the lake. I imagined I would fall if I did not seek support from something.

Now I was looking away from him and the table, out across the water. To my delight he took the necessary steps to join me; stood there adjacent, staring in the same direction. I wouldn't even incline my head, the better to view his shoulder or ribs. I sensed the warmth of his nudity next to me. I told myself I was being ridiculous, but that did not remove the bracken dryness from my mouth.

I could think of no specific words to continue a casual conversation with him. Inside my head beat the questioning refrain: Does he know? By either intelligence, understanding or brute instinct, *does he know?*

But there was something else active beneath my skull, too. That primitive awareness of danger. We stood close, I could almost experience him via *osmosis* — but there remained that crucial space between two men which might be physically invisible but was nevertheless as wide as the universe, the transgression of which could lead to major upheaval... danger... even sudden death.

"What you call me Carlos for?" he asked, addressing the sun-dancing lake. A fish plopped before I could manage a reply, sending a tiny spray of silvered water into the air.

"You reminded me of someone. From a long time ago." I thought my voice sounded disgustingly weak. Soft... too soft.

Apparently he did also. "The twins told me about you guys. You got another guy up there in Canada, right?"

I said nothing. What was there to say?

"I know who you are — don't try and deny it. Everyone around this lake knows you're queer."

How quickly the allure of his flesh dissolved! How speedily did the sense of him reshape as menace! "You seem to know an awful lot for one so young. It's a pity your grammar isn't equal to your gossip."

But there was to be no recovery of rôle — as houseguest, as a stranger who had been out there on the deck before he turned up, or even in the guise of a portly, middle-aged gent. He was now openly contemptuous. I did momentarily wonder what I might have said to precipitate this abrupt change in mood. But there was scant time for such reflection as he started then to verbally abuse me.

"If my friends knew you were here now they'd be right over. They sure don't like queers any more than me. Not since we had that math teacher at New Brunswick High."

I still tried to retrieve, if not poise, at least levity. "I can't even do math — let alone teach it."

He ignored me. "You shoulda seen that guy when we was through with him! A friend of mine said we turned a fucking fairy into a goddam gnome. How about that, huh?"

It was my time for silence.

"That Carlos? That some guy you blew when you was staying here before?"

"You've little sense of me," I said coldly. "Then that's hardly surprising."

He proved impervious to sarcasm. In fact he changed the subject entirely. Or so I initially thought. "Ten bucks isn't much for mowing a lawn, you know."

I was minded to suggest he take that up with the Polawskis, but a fresh glance at that savage slit of a mouth restrained me. We were alone out there, on a suburban, weekday morning, when all other homes in the vicinity were not only screened by the fresh foliage but had their occupants — if any — working indoors.

I noticed his hands again. They looked even larger than they had at first. Come to that, his erstwhile satin skin was now merely a hard sheath encasing a lot of muscle. With a new sense of despondency I realized I would be quite powerless if that animal body moved in aggression against me.

I imagined a winded stomach. (I'd been around in my own New York teenage past and knew all about gays being rolled.) I even took time out to imagine my denture smashing under the impact of his scornful hand; my reading glasses trodden to fragments on the deck. I sighed aloud. Why the hell had I even bothered to chat with him in the first place when surrounded by these vulnerable appendages of middle age?

Incongruously, over the years and over the thousands of watery miles that had separated us even in life, I heard my mother's scornful Cornish voice pronouncing over some aging Lothario in our village, that "there was no fool like an old fool." Was there ever a bigger fool than the one standing there now in suburban New Jersey being threatened and abused by some neighborhood kid?

"You still haven't answered my question."

I started in surprise — both at the force of his comment and the content of it. "What question?"

"How much I should get for cutting their goddam lawn. More than a tenner, right?"

"How the hell should I know," I said, surprised at my sullen tone. "I don't know the rates around here for things like that."

"I should get more," he insisted, now looking hard at me. "I want more."

"Then you'll have to take that up with the Polawskis, won't you?" If I felt sulky it was because I could see only too clearly, the end of this particular road.

"Gimme another fifty. I know you got it 'cos I saw it there."

"Of course I shall tell the Polawskis, you realize, that they've hired a punk. A thief."

"Arguin' just puts my rates up. Let's see what you got." His hand suddenly reached out and grabbed my left wrist. He twisted the skin beneath his clenched fingers. It hurt. I noticed that he glanced back towards the scattered houses behind the leafy scrim, just as I had a few moments earlier. But like me, he, too, was satisfied that we were unwatched.

With my free hand I took out my wallet once again. Only then did he let my wrist go. As slowly as I could I removed the first bill. Leadenly I noted it was a twenty — then recalled that all the smaller denominations were at the other end of the wad.

"Gimme all of it," the young man ordered.

"Let me keep something," I pleaded. That's all I brought with me from Canada."

"That's your fuckin' business. Here — let's have it."

But I held on. I don't know what exactly I intended to do. But there was just something in me that hesitated at such absolute passivity. Boldly I withdrew another twenty dollar bill — brushing aside his outstretched fingers to do so.

"Here," I said, as firmly as I was able. "Now take this and that's it. You needn't bother about my mentioning that to the Polawskis. You can have it as a gift. Then just bugger off. I don't want anything more to do with you."

The look he vouchsafed me contained an intensity of contempt I never wished to ever encounter again. "I don't take gifts from queers. But I want all you got there in your wallet. I deserve it for standing here letting your fruity eyes look at me, you fairy. And I'm going to have it, see?"

"Why all the name-calling?" I asked. "What the hell have I ever done to you? Jesus! Here I was, minding my own business until you came and stood there under those trees."

He didn't argue. Perhaps he felt at a disadvantage with words and discussion. Nevertheless he exploded, his rage laced with despisal of my presence. "Jesus H. Christ! The fuckin' world's gone to shit. Me and my buddies can't walk down a street in New Brunswick without being attacked by the niggers. And fruits like you everywhere! Oh shit! Gimme the money — I gotta get out of here!"

"Poor little middle-class white boy," I sneered — with a courage snatched from god-knows-where.

"The money," he hissed frantically. Then he bunched up the side of my shirt in his clenched hand and pushed me hard against the rail of the dock so that I was looking south to the further shore again.

"See that row boat? That's got my uncle and his pal aboard. If you don't give me that money quick I'm going to holler that you tried to put the make on me. I'll hit you first, you bastard, don't worry about that. But that's nothing to what *they'll* do to you when they get over here. I told you everyone on the lake knows what the Polawskis got staying with 'em."

I looked out at the metal skiff, to the spot where the two men who had rowed lazily past me, were now fishing. I had no way of knowing whether the kid was lying as to whether one of them was his uncle or not. But I suddenly felt too exhausted to call his bluff. Tired, that was, in ancticipation of all the humiliating explanations which would be subsequently needed.

Wordless, now, I handed him all the money in my hand. He didn't bother to count it but stuffed it into his own billfold. Mechanically, I slipped my now much slimmer wallet back whence it had come. The chocolate brown cover of Davis Grubb's novel, *Fool's Parade*, lying on the slatted table-top beckoned but did not welcome me. I saw small caterpillars, translucent green, hoop pliant bodies along the red-painted rail. And as I moved instinctively away from him, to sit down dejectedly on the paint-flaking bench, I felt caterpillar threads brush unpleasantly against my forehead and face.

"Bugger off!" I said, meaning this time, I think, the threads, or spiders' webs, or whatever they were. But he obviously thought I was repeating the injunction for his benefit.

"Fuck you, too," he muttered. Nevertheless he turned away towards the incline leading up to the back of the house.

I listened to his shoes in the gravel: I refused to watch his retreating, naked back. Instead I closed my eyes and thought of the lies I would invent for the Polawskis on their return — and sadly wondered how long would have to elapse before I could afford the whole truth with them.

I HATE QUEERS

I was early when I went to interview Kingston Mann, the distinguished westcoast photographer who lived in the same area that Malcolm Lowry had once known well. So early in fact that I walked across the Indian Reservation where every surname seemed to be that of 'George', looked in the direction of Deep Cove, and thought of Lowry. Not only of Lowry but his wife, Marjorie, and all those bottles of gin about which my friend, Murdoch McGregor, has so cheerfully regaled me as rationalization of his own prodigious boozing.

It was a late September morning, of that particular kind which makes coastal British Columbia sparkle in dew and brings bright globules of moisture against the dark bark of cedar and fir. Squeezing between bramble bushes, now mainly denuded of blackberries, I responded pleasurably to the gossamer knitting of spiders — their tracery on fire in the sun's long rays. Perhaps there was a hint of melancholy accompanying the autumnal nip in the air but I felt buoyed by the protraction of summer rather than dejected by the death of a season as I walked slowly down the track surrounded by tall clumps of salmonberry and salal and the grimmer green sprawl of oregon grape.

A Steller's jay flawed the silence as it broke into the brightness of Indian Arm where the water lay as blue as the sky above, and a large tanker rode incongruously at anchor before proceeding to the squat oil refinery below Burnaby Mountain. But there was no other sound save my feet on twigs. I thought fleetingly of the complexities of life back home in Kitsilano; of knotty financial problems and the endless striving to secure reputation — and was glad to stand where I did in the simplicity of morning.

I found a log, at the forest's edge, where I could look out across the mudflats where herons stalked and mergansers huddled in post-dawn stupor. There were other waterfowl and I wished I had brought my Audubon Field Guide. But that, I reflected, would have formalised the enterprise, diluting it of charm.

I took out a Matinee cigarette, lit it, and inhaled deeply — procuring a corresponding cough. For those interested in such matters, the action indicates that I was not yet five and forty, for that was the age I abandoned the practise permanently. It was also the period that a substantial portion of my income derived from interviewing established artists in all the various disciplines.

Discontent was not exactly my dominant mood as I sat there, the log dankly cool beneath the cords which clothed my backside, smoking pensively. Bored perhaps? Certainly those middle years, which I had just begun to experience, represented little that was overly dramatic. No more trans-continental decampments from home to home (with the concommitant lugging of chattels), no more wearing of uniforms for the admirals and generals; no more changing of nationalities or sitting for exams. Here I was, a middle-aged Canadian citizen, 'married' in spirit if not in law, and professionally competent in the kind of literary journalism which I had honed in London, New York and San Francisco before settling finally in Vancouver and doing the same thing for the media there.

If there was any emotional *Sturm und Drang* in my life of 1975 it was *vicariously* there: a borrowed thing from the dramatic calibrations of temperature in the lives and relationships of some of my younger and more fiery companions. Friend Murdoch, for instance. Murdoch McGregor of the vodka and gin bottles, one separated wife, two concurrent girlfriends, and a penchant for professional sex picked up in The Penthouse. Handsome Murdoch who so cheerfully shared his Simon Fraser University pay checks and who danced so vigorously in the glow of inebriated affection but who limped so forlornly when the hour was late, the bottle empty, and only male me stood as sterile consolation.

It had been Murdoch who had initially hinted I interview Kingston Mann. They had once worked together on a National Film Board documentary about the burgeoning Portuguese community in the south Okanagan valley (McGregor is a sociologist) but I don't believe his suggestion had anything to do with that. My friend had once dropped the information that Kingston Mann was as big a womanizer as he was, and would thus present a particular challenge as an interview subject to an invert like myself. Murdoch was a great one for challenges to his friends as — to be fair — he was for himself. As example of the latter, he once gave his two current bed-partners copies of a recent novel — and then grilled them on alternate nights as to their reactions. He had been delighted when, not unnaturally given the length of the novel which I think was Saul Bellow's *Humboldt's Gift*, he sometimes confused his two readers and started questioning one girl about a chapter she had read earlier and over which she had already delivered her opinions. His secondary interrogation certainly aroused *her* suspicions he gleefully confessed, but he had somehow avoided detection of his persistent philandering until both had finished the book. He had also managed, he boasted, to conceal from both of them the fact he was copulating with each on successive days.

The anecdote had grown in the re-telling until one day I heard him refer to *four* women engaged with the same novel — all on successive nights in his bed, and still with no suggestion of his being caught out. When I was feeling particularly disgruntled or sought to deflate "Manic Murdoch" as I was then wont to call my friend of fifteen years, I'd savagely opine that his incessant bloody jokes, love-making, and alcoholic consumption, only attested to desperation and an inferiority-complex over people like me.

On finally quitting the log and making my way back to the Peugeot and subsequently Kingston Mann's house, it was with thoughts of the endearing yet exasperating Murdoch still flitting about my mind. What banished them was not the impact of our common connection but the fact the photographer was simply not to be found.

Out there in that semi-rural setting I did something which would not have occurred to me in the city. After shouting Mann's name a couple of times and discovering his front door was unlocked, I went inside in search of him. Only I was careful to call out his name at frequent intervals. Room after room proved empty — although there were numerous signs of recent occupancy: empty coffee cups and eggstained breakfast plates on the kitchen table, butt-filled ashtrays everywhere; a sock in the corner of the living room and lots more clothes scattered about the bedroom, including a rather excessive number, I felt, of intimate female garments...

I was quick to notice that on the walls of all five or six rooms I entered there were numerous examples of the owner's highly distinctive nature photography. The kind of works that had earned him comparison with the likes of Edward Weston and Ansel Adams down in California.

It was my understanding that he was both married and a father but I came across neither wife nor children in my exploration. There was lipstick on a coffee cup which I took to be from his wife as both that and the size of the woman's underwear I'd noticed seemed incongruous in the context of the two little girls that Murdoch had mentioned.

When I finally walked out of that house I nursed an odd sense of being unclean as a result of my trespass. Gloomy, too. Of course, there is something about stale human debris which is invariably depressing, but the congealed *detritus* from a consumed breakfast and unmade beds in excessively untidy bedrooms evoked a sense of desolation which didn't depart as I looked towards the bush and snow-capped mountains of the Northshore beyond.

Mood aside, I still felt impelled to cast about for my would-be interview subject. I had driven some thirty kilometers to meet him and, besides, apart from a certain Celtic tenacity, I needed the money the article would eventually yield. I noticed a path between large clumps of scrub willow, leading northwards and decided to at least give that a try before giving up.

Rather surprisingly, it seemed, I was quickly out of sight, not only of Mann's house, but the surrounding evidences of patchy suburban development. I knew, as any Vancouverite would, that I was on the brink of the Great Wilderness and that beyond those uncertain settlements I had just left behind, there were no other major urban centers of the proportions of the city at the mouth of the Fraser until far past the Bering Straits and Soviet Siberia. Only a year or so earlier the skeleton of an Englishwoman, a vacationing teacher from Liverpool, had been discovered four months after she had failed to return from a weekend hike — and with no mark of foul play about her remains. And there are always those unfortunates, stripped bare of rotting flesh by bear and cougar, raven and bald-eagle, who having lost their way are never found whole.

It was not that I felt I was beginning to penetrate some Pacific coast equivalent of a jungle with its attendant hazards — as so incessantly clichéd by television. But I did have a notion of my puny self traversing an impervious immensity, and even of unseen life deep within that thickening screen of vegetation, that did not welcome my presence. The walking got more difficult as the track narrowed and the yellowing leaves and moist twigs progressively whipped my cheeks. The silence of the place, however, gradually gave place to a faint but insistent chatter from an invisible stream off to my right. The climb was now steady and in spite of the fact the fall sun wasn't all that fierce, the sweat began to trickle from my hairline. My smoker's lungs wheezed, too.

I was relieved when I reached a small clearing where the stream suddenly put in an appearance as a border to the track up which I had been laboring. I slumped down on a spread of coarse twitch grass which the sun of the past summer had dried to hay. I looked wearily about me. My languor abruptly drained and I was tense and alert again. I had the prickly impression of being watched — although I had no idea from which direction.

But no one materialized as I sat there, knees hunched up to my chin, my hands clasped about them. Growing tired of staring fruitlessly into dense foliage or towards remote snowcaps, I looked upwards instead. Two eagles soared in circles, their blunt wings majestic in size and in their command of the air. I envied those birds: not just their mastery of the thermal currents, but their fantastic sight which would not have shared my difficulty in discerning whether I was being spied on. I knew those eagles could see me — in spite of their altitude in that azure atmosphere. And at the same time I sensed more than ever that, joined to the scrutiny of their yellow, avian eyes, were two human ones...

I clambered back to my feet and continued up the steep path, calling out the name of Kingston Mann every now and then. It met with no response. The vegetation when I estimated I'd covered at least three kilometers from Mann's home, was noticeably more sparse and was superseded by increasingly large patches of shale and outcropping on either side of the now truly turbulent stream in its shallow gulch. Instead of the almost forest of small trees there were just isolated stands of saplings with little grass or weeds underfoot. The fall colors were less defined up here.

I arrived at an enormous boulder which at first I thought blocked my way — until I realized that the narrow path wound right around it, taking me almost to the edge of the frothing water. I took my time traversing the rock, clinging to its lichen-furred sides and trying not to look down at the spume-strewn torrent.

After I had successfully accomplished the manoeuvre I did look back — in small triumph at my rudimentary mountaineering. It was also partly, I guess, to see if I was being followed. It was as well that I did so. For the first time since embarking on what I was beginning to conclude was a stupid and unprofitable hike, I had vivid evidence of human activity: freshly executed and close to hand. With the use of a spray-can, across the immense face of the boulder and on its north side had been emblazoned the curt statement:

I HATE QUEERS

Slowly, trancelike — for I think my head was void of coherence — I moved back towards the slogan, my hand outstretched. My fingers met the bold white paint. It was drippingly wet. I glanced quickly about me once more, finally certain I had a malevolent companion. Further up the stone-littered path there were a number of fragmented rocks, many of them large enough to impede a car or small truck. As I scrutinized them I saw a sudden flash of color between two of the biggest. It was the briefest glimpse but I knew by the shade of red that it was no animal lurking there.

I didn't budge but stood motionless beneath the savage slogan. "I can see you! Come on out!" And when there was no reply. "Don't be such a coward!"

Only then did the figure of a man fully materialise and start walking down the path by the rolling waters in my direction. Long before he reached me I was sure it was Kingston Mann. The photographer was not a tall guy but his physique suggested power and a lot of energy. His shoulders — what I could discern under the red plaid Pendleton shirt — were unusually broad and the thick thighs in his jeans spelled strength, too. He had black, curly hair going slightly grey at the sides. He was a handsome bastard but not someone I would have liked to encounter in the dead of night. Dead of night? There was nothing reassuring about meeting him mid-morning in that remote place!

His manner proved as economical as his physical frame. To have called him taciturn would have been to put a fine point on it.

"Kingston Mann? I am Davey Bryant. I believe we had an appointment?"

I put out my hand — although the gesture was at variance with my inner feelings. I need not have bothered. He ignored it.

"Yes I am."

"You sprayed this behind me on the rock, didn't you?"

"Yes I did."

"Why, for God's sake?"

He shrugged those broad shoulders. "I felt like it."

"Was — was it meant for me?"

"If the cap fits..." He tailed off.

My fear of the man sprang an angry inflection in my voice.

"That's a bit much, isn't it? After all, I'm a complete stranger. You know nothing whatever about me."

Kingston Mann plonked himself down heavily on a flattish stone right opposite to where I stood.

"McGregor told me all about you."

I mentally cut Murdoch's disloyal throat.

"Then why, for Chrissake, agree to the interview? I was at your place dead on ten — just as we'd agreed over the 'phone."

He seemed quite unabashed. "I started thinking about things before you were due. And — well — I decided I didn't want to see you after all."

"Think about what *kind* of things?" I had intended that to sound business-like. After all, this sonofabitch had brought me on a wild goose chase and wasted my morning. But the words came thick and whiny and I tasted shame.

I knew why, of course. When your sexual cover is blown before a stranger — for people like me it is hard to regain equilibrium. Even so, I persevered. It didn't look now as if he were going to physically assault me. And my earlier anxiety that perhaps whoever was out there watching me from the deep of the scrub might be carrying a gun (the result of too much TV I guess) had by now evaporated. I decided to brazen it out.

But he simply wasn't interested in anything I might say or do. "It's not you as an individual so much. I might even like you — then again, I might not. But what you people stand for sticks in my craw. And with over an hour and a half to think about it I decided not to be a hypocrite for once. I hoped, though, you'd just knock a couple of times, get the message, and then be on your way."

"What I *stand* for," I said hotly, "is me! I'm not a goddamn cause! Unless, of course, you have biblical objections to meeting me. Then I gathered from our mutual friend Murdoch McGregor that Kingston Mann, the photographer, was beyond the pygmy attitudes of a bunch of simplistic bible-punchers with their neatly selected texts." (And if I said that sneeringly, well and good!)

"It's got nothing to do with that. When I started out I wanted to be a fashion photographer. The Condé Nast organisation? Vogue Magazine? I learned the truth in New York in less than two weeks! You guys had everything sewn up. Fairysville wasn't in it! Later I found it was the same in all the arts. You give one another jobs whether you're any good or not. Look at the C.B.C. for Chrissakes! But for years now, I've gone on making the right little liberal noises and saying queers are just like everyone else. Well, buster, I'm up to here with that crap." (He made a suitable gesture with his hand before his throat.) "Just for once I'm going to try the truth with myself, whatever it costs. And that, by the way, includes my wife who took off in a snit with the kids this morning when I told her I wasn't going to be interviewed. You guys have plenty of allies with women like her."

But I wasn't about to reduce matters to where I became merely a bit of ammunition between a warring husband and wife. "Why stop with us?" I asked icily. "So we stick together just like the Jews. And did you ever notice that we got rhythm and big dongs as well? After all, there's no need to let the Darkies off the hook, is there?" I leaned back against the defaced boulder as I sought fresh words for attack. "It's really a pity I can't offer you Jewish blood and a touch of the tarbrush. Then you could at least lump all your prejudices in one basket."

"Don't be smart," he said slowly. "I've got nothing against Jews or Blacks. It's *queers* I'm talking about, Mr. Davey Bryant. Homos, fags, inverts, pooftas — that's the crowd I detest. And provided I don't persecute any one, I have a perfect right to my likes and dislikes. As a matter of fact I already feel a hundred per cent better for getting that off my chest. It's better than using a spray can. I'm glad you followed me up here. But that's it — game's over. Now will you kindly fuck off?"

He looked down towards his large work boots. I sensed he wasn't going to even look in my direction again. I squirmed under his scorn. "I'm really sorry for you," I muttered. "My God, you're a mess!"

He remained silent. I drew in deep breath. At least I'd gotten in the last word. I suppose to refuel my righteous indignation, I turned and stole a final glance at the words in white paint. The rivulets had increased their descent. The word QUEERS now looks much more like QUEENS. In spite of myself, I smiled at that. How many times in a bar had I heard some uptight gay say "I hate queens!"

But I made bloody certain that Kingston Mann didn't see my grin before I started to walk stiffly away with whatever dignity I was able to muster.

5

INSIDE OUT

There was fall mist along the Burnaby slopes of the Fraser River when I drove out to Oakalla prison to visit young Fred Oliphant — house burglar, drug-store robber and general roustabout in beer parlors and bars. He was twenty, my junior by fifteen years; an Ottawa Valley boy from Carleton Place who was relatively new to the coast. These facts were in my possession before I ever met him. They had been furnished by the prison doctor who thought that by bringing us together, Fred's literary ambitions might be served — and that my own experience could be broadened. Murray Hollingsworth, a Fourth Avenue shopping acquaintance was ever anxious to liberate me from an ivory tower. I am not sure to what degree either goal was realized, but if I lay out the details you might arrive at your own conclusions.

I went through all the time-consuming activity of a visitor's entry; caused the same loud clanging of steel doors, the clicking and unclicking of locks, and shouts of the various guards as I progressively penetrated the bowels of the jail. Eventually I found myself in the company of a sullen man in tan uniform outside Cell 4 in the Young Offenders Unit (Westgate A) at the Provincial Correctional Centre. It was late September, 1969.

Fred Oliphant's skin was of a pallor suggesting illness and his hair was straight to the point of spikiness. It was prison short, conforming to then current prison practice, and far from profuse. His eyes were shifty in the manner institutions make them, and the main distinguishing feature above the slim, stooped body, was the absence of two upper front teeth — remarkable, I thought, in one so young. This caused him to lisp slightly and although there was not a trace of effeminacy about the figure slumped on the lower tier of his otherwise empty cell, the dental gaps and consequent sibilance contributed to an overall image of frailty and sickness. I warmed at once to the combination. I knew that he had already been over a year in Oakalla, that he had previously done three years in Saskatchewan, and that his father, an alcoholic, had recently died. These things obliging Murray Hollingsworth had told me as we had waited to be served in Jackson's, the butchers. What the good doctor had *not* told me was how mat-skinned and dull-eyed Fred Oliphant was — nor of the egregious whine, born I presumed, of years of prison life when to wheedle from the 'screws' was the only alternative to bullying your fellow inmates if you had the prowess and clout.

He was very nervous with me at first. He shoved a bundle of creased and much scrawled-on graph paper in my direction, after we had introduced ourselves and the guard had stepped outside, closed the door and opened the spy-hole. Without looking up at me Fred explained the sheets of oft-smudged longhand.

"Poems, they are. I do stories, too. One of 'em is in the pile, I think. Prob'ly no good but like Doc Hollingsworth says, I was to show you all I done."

"I'll be pleased to read through them, Fred. The doctor told me how impressed he was."

"I wrote 'em late at night. I got no diction'ry. The spellin' is all wrong. But he said to give 'em to you as they was."

"Exactly. We can fix them up afterwards."

"Like I write 'em when I can't sleep? Sometimes I'm on medication. Jesus! They sure fly out of me then! I often write poems when I'm high. Like it helps when I'm feeling a need for the medication. You get like that, eh? I mean on a downer and that?"

"Of course. We all do, I guess."

I terminated the conversation shortly after that. Putting it all together you might say I was not overly impressed by Mr. Oliphant. But I can't say the same over that sheaf of dishevelled pages which I read and re-read before turning off the light to sleep that night. Some of them contained magic.

Nevertheless, excited though I was during succeeding weeks by the growing pile of papers with his poems and prose-reflections scrawled upon them, I cannot honestly say I knew a commensurate increase in my respect or admiration for him as a person. At the first mild gesture of encouragement on my part, a reference to his artistic strengths, an allusion to his youth, to the future promise for such a prodigious talent, he would turn to the ills that soured his every waking moment and made his sleep a festering chain of nightmares. The complaints sounded credible enough in their individual context but in endless, repetitious aggregate they threatened my sanity. From a sitting position on the seatless toilet bowl opposite his bunk, where he sprawled in monotonous lament, I would turn to pacing up and down the tiny cell — as if it were mine and I the inmate.

There was one other strand to his plaintive stream that didn't materialize until the first few weeks of visiting had elapsed. It was the subject of *parole*. But once he had brought it up it was invariably there — along with the sickly lauding of me and the endless self-vindication over his prison term.

There was the space of a month or so after the holidays when I refused to make the drive out to Oakalla at all. I had enough on my plate, what with Ken distracted by term-paper and exam marking at the University of British Columbia, the jealousy of a fellow-writer on the newspaper, and the generally lousy January weather, to make the prospect of listening to Fred's cracked phonograph record frankly insupportable.

Then guilt began to build in me — with a final twist of conscience supplied by a chance encounter with Dr. Hollingsworth in our local Safeway.

"I gather you've given up on young Oliphant," he said right off.

"Can't blame you. He really is a bit of a menace."

"He knows how to write," I said reluctantly, wishing the subject would go away. "But he does tend to go on."

"I wouldn't know anything about the literary stuff. That's your department. But I did say he was a bit of a manipulator. You did know what you were letting yourself in for." With that the portly prison doctor helped himself to a can of lobster chowder. I thought of Fred's unerring ability to irritate me. "I wouldn't say he was a very *good* manipulator," I said slowly. "In fact he's absolutely lousy!"

Hollingsworth shrugged, then reached down to add a crab bisque can to his shopping cart. "Depends what he wants. He gets his full share of medication. It's the only way to shut him up."

"He hasn't been given a parole, though. That's what he wants most," I said.

"Didn't even know he was eligible. They're always changing the fool rules. Never brought it up with me. Too busy getting his pills, I guess."

"Well, it amazes me!" I couldn't keep the incredulity out of my voice. "And I can asure you that he does want parole. He feels he'll write a whole lot better when he's off drugs, for one thing."

"If you really think it will help him and I think he's ready for it, I'll certainly suggest it in my next report."

"When would he be free?" I asked quickly.

"It's not an overnight business. If it's granted at all it would be several months, I imagine, being processed."

I relaxed. "If there is anything I can do to help speed it up, just let me know," I said.

It was yet another month before I saw Fred again. Even before I had crossed the threshhold of his cell I knew that something momentous had happened. The ends of his mouth were turned up rather than down as usual. He was brisker in his movements, and paced and circled the cell before I had time to perch on the toilet bowl. He didn't keep me in suspense.

"I gotta hearing," he announced. "Board's goin' to look into my case. Doc says I got a bloody good chance if everything goes right."

His eyes, which seemed more green than blue in the harsh cell light, also looked fresh and clear. Besides, they looked straight at me for a change. I sensed he was brimming with excitement and expectancy. It didn't even occur to me to feel relieved that he had dispensed with the fulsome praise or his gripes over the trial. Instead I felt suddenly encouraged; glad that I didn't know the urge to distinguish between his person and his poems.

"What does 'everything' mean, Fred?"

"I gotta have bread for when I get out and I gotta have a job to go to. Say, have I gotta pile of stuff for you! I been busy, Man!"

He smiled as he handed me a voluminous bundle of paper covered with the now familiar scrawl of his pencilled hand. I started to reassemble the sheets but in fact I wasn't really examining them at all. I was just thinking very quickly. "I can't make too many promises but I'll certainly ask people to help with the job and the money. How much cash do they want?"

"Couple hundred bucks should take care of it. Check with Admin. on the way out, why dontcha?" And possibly, just because that sounded a little too much like an order, "Thanks, Dave. There's no one I could ask, see. Like I don't know no one else out there."

There was a forlorn note to those final words which I carried all the way home with me. It continued to prod as I made up a list of people whom I might ask for cash to help spring Fred. It nudged me, too, when I made out a second, longer list, of potential employers.

Phase one was achieved with gratifying speed. Just one telephone call and Lawrence Myers was saying to me: "It's about time I put something back into the kitty. God knows, I've taken plenty out. Will $500 be enough for the poor bastard?"

On the other hand, I'd crossed out nine names and February had turned into March before I secured a definite promise to take on my inmate when he got out. It wasn't much of a job either. A friend who was night-manager at a downtown hotel offered work involving hauling soiled linen to the laundry.

Before Tony Gill agreed (reluctantly at that) to see Fred about this menial employment. I received a letter via Murray Hollingsworth from Oakalla enclosing yet more poems and a sentimental, not to say, unoriginal, story about a mouse in a prison cell. The story is now mercifully lost, Fred took the poems with him, and only the letter now remains in my possession.

> Dear Davey:
> I guess you've forgot all about me. Don't blame you as this place is meant for forgotten men. That's the way these fuckers want it. Out of sight, out of mind, eh? But I keep on writing, just like you told me. Here is something to prove it. All I done to the present. Do what you like with them. All they is to me now is reminders of when I can't sleep at nights. When I have to have the medication that Doc Hollingsworth don't give me without a fight. You'd think he owns the bloody pills when we wants them what can't sleep however much we tries. I reckon you've probably forgotten about poor old Fred by now. With the better weather around you can see a bit of blue sky from my window. But don't hold your breath as the new spring leaves will blot out the sky again.
> It is worse now than it was before for me in here, Dave, as I know I could have that parole if I had the bread and someone would line up a job. It don't matter how small the cash what goes with it. But you are a busy writer I know. I am just

someone rotting away in a goddamn cage where these bastards would like to see me forever.

Broken-hearted and full of depression which even the medication don't help any more. I remain your old prison friend,

Frederick Percy Oliphant.

That letter twisted my entrails. I would have gone out to the prison as soon as possible but, in any case, the grudging promise from my hotel contact arrived that same week. So I was able to see him, after the long absence, with positive information on both counts. I gave him no opportunity to spoil the occasion with a boring torrent of complaint. Before he had crossed to me from the barred window where he was standing on tiptoe, I told him I'd raised the cash and landed a job. For an unforgettable moment as he crossed the bare cell floor I thought he was going to embrace me. Kiss me. But his hand reached out just before we would have collided. I jerked mine up to grasp it.

"I can't thank you enough, Dave," he muttered. "Jeeze, I thought you'd forgot. I asked Doc every time but he just said how busy you was." He paused a moment. "I could be out in a month. Two at the latest. Think of that!"

I did. All the way home to Kits, through the soft spring greenery, I thought of Fred Oliphant and of the new life in the coastal city that now awaited him.

We got him a basement apartment on Kitsilano Point with small windows almost level with the lawn. There were flower beds beyond and a sanded path bi-furcating the twin strips of grass. It was a cheap rent and wholly unfurnished. But after two weeks of diligent attendance at local auction rooms Ken and I managed to make the place look quite habitable.

Fred was due to be released on a Saturday and as I had already written to him and provided the address, we decided to give him a surprise house-warming at his new home. As guests we invited Larry Myers and his wife, and Tony Gill who would hopefully be his new boss.

It was by now late April and the Chinese grocery stores in the neighborhood had their sidewalks ablaze with color where their owners had pails of cut-flowers arranged in tiers before their windows. There were not just the expected freesias and stocks, anemones, iris and carnations. There were also sprigs of mimosa, huge bunches of purple and white lilac and some clumps of chestnut branches with creamy cones and pale leaves.

I went slightly mad and bought everything in sight. To prevent Fred's place looking like a funeral parlour we had eventually to take a good third of my purchases back with us to decorate our own home. Even so, there was hardly a flat surface in that basement apartment which didn't have some display of flowers or floral shrubs decorating it.

One of the auction 'finds' was an inexpensive card table and this we covered with a bright Italian tablecloth of red and yellow squares, which Ken unearthed from the napkin closet under the kitchen counter.

We met at noon. That is, Ken and I and the Meyers did. Tony was fifteen minutes late. But we were all assembled before Fred's arrival, and sat around to wait. By 1 p.m. there was no sign of him and by 1:30 p.m. it occurred to me that he might not appear. The others had left by mid-afternoon and we then collected the remnants of gin and sherry, wine and our candlesticks and returned home.

It wasn't until the following Wednesday that I received a phone call from an errant Fred who was apparently calling from a transient hotel on the edge of skid row. My voice was cold and my response to his cheerful greeting a series of sharp questions about the date of his release and what he'd been up to in the interim. None of which he answered specifically or in any way satisfactorily. He let me do most of the talking but I wasn't really aware of the fact until I petered out and he offered no response. It was during the ensuing silence that I realized that his voice — what little I'd heard of it — sounded different from when I'd last heard it in the confines of his cell. The difference was subtle; a new hoarseness and a crisper tone. But it was real, nevertheless.

"Yeah, well like I had some business to do first. Guess I forgot to tell you. I didn't think it would take so long." He'd paused then before adding significantly: "Or turn out so expensive, Dave."

"The place we chased around for and eventually found for you is still waiting," I told him. "And that, too, will prove expensive if you don't get your tail over there and start using it. I should add you spoiled a celebration lunch, wasted an afternoon for five people and disappointed those who had put out most for you. But as I say the place is still there — if you still want it, of course." I didn't bother to conceal my sarcasm.

"You got the key? Of course I want my own pad. Think I'm stupid?"

"I was beginning to think so," I told him. "Look, I'll drive down and meet you at the apartment. I can shop for us on the way." There was no answer on the line. "Hello? You still there?"

A tired voice (or was it bored?) then answered me. "Sure I'm here. See you at the apartment then. Number 1806, right?"

When I drove up, expecting to nip in and make sure everything was neat and welcoming — I had brought fresh syringa from our yard — it was to find Fred already waiting. "God! You made that quickly! Got a good connection on the bus?"

He shrugged and stood there a trifle impatiently outside the front door. "Taxi," he muttered. "I didn't want to wait around there no longer."

I held back the impulse to comment on his extravagance, then brushed past him to unlock the dark green door, and handed him the yale key. I went straight to the large vase in which wilted lilac rusted, and took it across to the sink to replace it with the fragrant mock-orange I'd brought with me. I returned the smoked glass vase to the cardtable and in doing so noticed that Fred was already sprawled in the single armchair, using the telephone which Ken had generously paid for to be installed and rented for the first month. "Yeah, well, like I gotta split, Lou. Be talkin' to you, huh?"

He let the receiver crash loudly back into its cradle. "It's good to see you so relaxed," I commented. I certainly never did in Oakalla, that's for sure!"

His response was immediate. He jumped up to his feet and commenced to pace the basement room. I wished at once I'd not mentioned the prison.

"Those bastards will never see me back in there — I swear to God, Davey." The look he threw me was not of desperation. More of defiance. His mobile mouth was not turned down and there was no lack of focus in those blue-green eyes. I'm not sure I liked what I saw.

"It's entirely up to you, isn't it? You know the terms of your parole, I don't. By the way, I've left you our number and address on that piece of paper — in case you've already lost it. Call me when you're settled and I'll come down and fetch you. No need to take taxis in this part of town. Ken and I thought we'd give you supper, seeing it's your first night, more or less."

Fred paused in his criss-crossing the threadbare carpet. "Mind if I take a raincheck? I guess I'm pretty beat. I should make it an early night before I go see that guy about the hotel job. Want to be my best, don't I?"

It was my turn to shrug. "As you please." I concealed my disappointment. After Fred had phoned I'd immediately called some friends and asked them to dinner. But I had to admit that they would understand if I explained that our parolee was having a little problem adjusting.

He followed me to the door. "Just one other thing, Dave. Could you let me have car fare for tomorrow morning?"

"Jesus!" I remonstrated. "What happened to the five hundred dollars?"

"In the bank," he said quickly — too quickly. "I spent what little change I had on the cab. I'll draw some more tomorrow — like when I know the job's in the bag and that."

With reluctance I pulled a dollar bill from my wallet. "I'm sorry I haven't anything smaller," I said, handing it over. And I really was.

All the way home I was bothered by Fred. Something nagged like a soft but persistent buzzer. I felt prickly with unease, especially over handing him the money — even if it was such a paltry sum. I finally put it down to the notion that he still bore the aura of prison about him — an institution where even the sunlight was laced with suspicion and all motives perceived as ulterior. I vowed I would never lend him a single cent ever again. That made me feel much better...

The next day Tony called to say he had been most impressed by Fred and would be only too glad to take him on his limited payroll. We invited

Fred to supper as his evenings would be less free in the future. This time
he quickly and enthusiastically accepted. I was particularly content to
observe that he and Ken got on famously from the outset. Fred was much
more relaxed with my roommate, I noticed, and behaved almost as if
Ken were a respected older brother. I suspected he perceived me in a
more custodial light. Indeed, so readily did the two of them laugh and
chat in easy camaraderie that I have to confess to a spasm of jealousy
which I knew was quite stupid. In consolation I reminded myself that it
was I who had followed up on Murray Hollingsworth's suggestion and
discovered the indubitable talents of this strange young poet, and that I
was already arranging the publication of three of his works in a prairie-
based magazine.

I informed Fred of this good news when we were all three in the process
of washing up the dinner things. His response, verbally at least, was
wholly apt: the personal thanks, the enquiry as to the calibre of the
magazine and its editor, his delight at public recognition. But there was
something missing in spite of the words. Something to do, perhaps, with
an absence of the kind of emotional keening he had vouchsafed so readily
in prison over injustice and incarceration. It was a prison acomplishment
he seemed now to be referring to and not part of the new reality he sought
to embrace. Perhaps prison-poets, I reflected, are only that...

When Fred had been duly driven home and Ken and I were sitting
over a nightcap of scotch, I brought the matter up. Ken thought about
what I said for a while before replying. He usually does. "You could be
right, of course. He could want to put all the writing behind him. But
there's something else, Davey. He obviously hero worships you. It could
be that he wants to prove something about himself to you that was
impossible when he was just locked up and passive in jail."

"I'm not sure what you mean," I argued. "It was his poetry I liked in
the first place. As a person — well, you can see for yourself he's a little
difficult. Leaves something to be desired?"

"Just don't expect too much of him, that's all," Ken advised. "Now
that he's out, there's more potential to go wrong. It's like new gadgets on
cars." And with that cryptic assertion he rose, stubbed out a cigarette,
and declared he was ready for bed.

I had occasion to recall Ken's words just one week later. The jabbing of
memory came through a further phone call. Tony Gill from the Ritz
called to ask if I knew whether Fred was better and when he could be
expected to return to work. I didn't let on that I was quite ignorant of
what he was talking about but instead told Tony that I would check
things out and get back to him. But I didn't have to. Fred called that very
afternoon.

"I was just thinking about you," I said. "Tony was asking after you."

The pause was so slight that, had I not been suspicious, it would have
been imperceptible. "I was just trying to get you but the line was busy. I
only now got back from Nanaimo, see. From my sister's place."

"That is where you went for your convalescence then?"

This time I wasn't sure whether he missed my sarcasm or simply ignored it. "She was very ill. Norman — that's her husband — he thought she was dying. I took the first ferry I could. My sister and I was always very close. When I got there I learned she had pneumonia. Doctor says it was a miracle she come through. I haven't had time to do no writing, Dave. That's what I'm going to do this afternoon. So could you explain to Tony-boy and tell him I'll be at work tomorrow morning? I could do with an early night, too, after all I been through with ole Betty."

"You never mentioned any relatives in British Columbia. I thought they were all back in Ontario." I stopped abruptly, suddenly tired of all the shit he was feeding me. Anger surged where seconds before had been cultivated patience.

"You there, Davey?" The anxiety of the prison cell was back in the voice. I replaced the telephone, biting a lip already white from such pressure. "Fuck it!" I said to our standard poodle, Kim, who was watching me apprehensively from the sofa — wondering whether my anger was at his furniture trespassing, I suppose. "Fuck him! And fuck him again!"

Nor did ire subside with my decision to confront Fred with this new falsehood. I am not proud of the way I drove along Point Grey Road, wrenching the steering wheel left to turn onto Kitsilano Point and narrowly missing a cyclist (who gave me the finger) as I did so. Nor can I give rational defense to the sense of humiliation I felt at being duped. I told myself that my indignation was primarily on behalf of those I had begged to help Fred on his release, and whom he had betrayed, just as he had betrayed me. But it really went deeper than that. I remembered every little occasion he had let me down — and even some of those I had overlooked when they had occurred. How can I put it? It was a kind of violation: a sullying of the spirit such as the victims of robbery experience.

By the time I pulled up opposite the basement apartment I was literally shivering with a rage which had received further fuelling all the way from our place to his. I almost ran up the path. On either side the unmowed lawn now swayed with silver-eared hay. My assumption that the basement door was unlocked proved quite correct. I flung it open and remained there swaying in my wrath. Fred stood by the telephone, the directory open next to it. In spite of the outside warmth of that summer's day, it was pointedly cool in there. It also smelled damp from being a basement suite.

The tooth-gapped smile was instant. "Glad to see you, Dave ole pal. I tried to call you back when we was cut off. Then I thought p'raps you was refusing to answer me like."

It was contempt which finally cooled me. "I'm sure you did come to that conclusion. But by then I was on my way here. I'd made my decision."

Fred edged slowly away from the phone in my direction. Just a couple of steps. Then he paused. Spoke uncertainly. "Decision?"

"Not to listen to any more of your stupid lies. Not even to pretend to."

"What lies? I never told no lies to you, Dave. I couldn't. Not after all you done for me and that."

I slumped into the wicker chair furthest from him. Eyed him as he toyed with his hands which pendulummed about the front of his person. I noticed how his zipper was clearly visible along part of his fly; the tape holding it coming slightly apart from the material of his pants proper. It had happened to my own trousers — when I had grown fat and my pants too tight. Fred was very thin, though. So thin that his hands and feet seemed too large. Disproportionate.

"Sit down!" I ordered. "I want to talk to you. You'd better listen." Instead, he took a step closer to me. Now I could see clearly where the actual stitches of his zip track had come away. It was then I realized what he was doing with his hands in front of him. I took an even deeper breath. That removed a sudden dizziness. "Sit down!" I said again. Only this time I was close to shouting.

"Wha' for?" he muttered. "I never told you no lies." But he retreated, all the same. Back to the armchair by the telephone. He plonked himself down in it, heavily, his legs both stretched wide apart. "What the fuck's this all about, eh?"

I don't think I have ever felt so calm. Not only calm — Godlike. My controlled presence, my enormous will, filled the basement room. "I was showing someone your stuff," I began, carefully keeping all color from my voice. "When I next saw her on campus she had your poems to return. Only they were stuck in a book. The book, Fred, was called *The Sea Is Also a Garden*. It was an early volume of poems by Phyllis Webb."

"What the hell's that got to do with me?" He had crosed his legs and his left foot was twitching, as if not by his own volition.

I just went on: baritone calm. Remorseless: "I can't remember the exact words she quoted me but it was something about: *"We who have considered suicide take our daily walk with death and are not lonely."* The poem, by the way, was called *To Friends Who Have Also Considered Suicide*. She showed me the page and then the exact line in *your* suicide poem that you showed me the second time I came out to Oakalla."

"Those things happen. What they call it? Subconscious? I guess it just got in my mind without thinking too much about it. Then, when I was thinking of killing myself and writing about it — it just come out again. Happens all the time, Man, that kind of thing. You ask the Doc."

"I know, Fred, that if I went through all your stuff — line by line — I'd come across heaps more. I suspected it all the time. More than once. Just suppressed it, I suppose. Anyway, it isn't your stupid plagiarism that's brought me down here."

He honed in on that. "What you want to use long words like that on me? You just trying to put me down? I never did pretend I was educated like you."

"Since your release you've hardly levelled with me once. I know now why you didn't turn up when you were originally supposed to. And I know you just walked off the job with Tony. And please don't bother with any more lies about a sister in Nanaimo. So I'm really here to tell you we're through. You are on your own now — get that through your head. This is goodbye, Fred. Go see your parole officer. If you know his address, that is."

I thought that a congruous moment to stand up. And so did he. Only I did it to reinforce my authority, while I think he moved in panic more than anything else.

"You make me sick," he muttered, crossing swiftly to the door where his jacket hung. The move put me off balance. I was not expecting it.

"What the hell do you think you're doing now?" I asked.

"Goodbye, you said. Well I gotta blow. Goodbye, goodbye, goodbye." Suiting action to words, he yanked at the door as he thrust his arms through the sleeves of his newly acquired and expensive leather jacket. He kept moving, emerged into the sunlight and continued quickly down the path.

I was following him before he had even crossed the threshhold and caught up with him before he had attained the sidewalk. "You're being stupid again," I said to his shoulder. "You can't spend the whole of your life acting on impulse."

"I'm not going back," he replied. "No goddamn parole officer is going to put me back in the joint. I'll die first."

I wasn't even sure he was looking where he was going as he crossed the road and started to pass through the copse of maple and dogwood towards the sandy cliffs. The idea crossed my mind that perhaps he was going to slide down the scree, clamber over the low rocks, and enter the water to drown.

I drew parallel with him. "It's the lies that bother me. Not the goofing off. It's what bugs Ken, too."

He darted me a glance then. "What you told Ken?"

He was walking quickly, with a slight lurch. As if he were limping, although I had no reason to suspect him lame. Somehow, out there in the open, he seemed smaller, more vulnerable, than inside. It came to me that I habitually thought of him as someone confined to the space of his cell.

"I've told him everything. Then we always do. Not about your Nanaimo nonsense yet. He wasn't home when you made all that up about your sick sister."

"I do have a sister," he said sullenly.

I interrupted him before he could expound on that. "That was never under discussion. Let's just forget about her location, though."

"He knows about the poems? The ones I wrote in the joint?"

I noticed how he still carefully avoided all mention of plagiarism, and decided to ride with it. I accepted the fact that even if the Phyllis Webb lines were shoved under his nose, he would still go on denying it. Incontrovertible evidence in the courthouse or out was just an alien concept for Fred Oliphant. For all inmates as far as I knew.

"I told him that you didn't seem much interested in writing poetry any more, now that you were on the outside." (Somehow Fred's prevarications seemed to spawn a corresponding candour in me). "In fact he went on and told me not to expect too much from you at first as you would probably screw up a lot."

He didn't reply to that. Just took a right where the track forked and passed down a narrow path between sweet-smelling privet, towards the large V frame which housed the RCMP ship, the St. Roche. When beyond that he slackened his pace somewhat, for which I was grateful. By now I was not only aware of my extra fifteen years but my added fifty pounds!

"I like ole Ken," he said suddenly, breaking the silence again. "He don't say much but I reckon he understands me, ole Ken does."

"He hasn't had to put up with the shit from you that I have," I told him. "You've never tried to snow him like you have me." I could detect the self-pity in my words, however rough their delivery. I didn't like what I heard. I felt an abrupt flip-over of emotion towards my companion. Fred's company was rather like being on a rollercoaster with the dips and summits crowding one another in dizzying succession.

"If you'd only try and level with me just one little bit. It would be so much easier. It isn't too much to ask, is it?" I tried to read those greeny-blue eyes once more. But I couldn't be sure whether it was bafflement or cunning I saw there.

"Trouble is," he said slowly, "you're too much like the rest of 'em."

"Them?"

"That lot out there. Hollingsworth, the Chaplain, Father Wainwright. All of 'em!"

I was certain I could perceive contempt in his voice — whatever his eyes said. "I could say the same about you," I retorted, at once competitive.

"Whadja mean?"

"You're not the first con I've met, you know. I've visited Pentonville in London, and San Quentin in California."

"That's what I mean," Fred said. "You've got it all figured out, haven't you? You get a high by knowing people like me. It makes you groove to be a do-gooder. Bleedin'-hearts they call your type on them talk-in radio shows."

I was angry all over again. Jesus! This was the guy cringing and crawling for me to help him just a few short weeks ago! "When you lie to me, Fred, you insult me. It means you think I'm stupid enough to believe your crap. But I'm not one of your square-johns you think the world is composed of, except for the likes of smart-asses like you. I told you in Westgate A what I tell you now. The real dummies were those who stayed in their cells when I walked out. I'm smarter than you — that's the point."

He looked at me as if I were a thousand miles away. "O.K., o.k. Have it your way. So you're smarter. You gotta education, too. And you got bread. You got it all, Man. So how about lending me five bucks until I got this stuff with Pete settled and I get my pay cheque from his hotel?"

What I had just told myself was his arrogance in so nervily criticizing me, I now called his gall. And was proportionately milder in my response. I almost admired his cheek! I was beginning to have second thoughts about a total repudiation of him. I knew deep down I was being hypocritical. I simply didn't want to lose him — although I told myself it was because I had a moral obligation over his future. I most assuredly didn't allow a perverse sense of attraction towards him surface. Then I cannot be the only person constitutionally incapable of savouring a multiplicity of motivations at one and the same time.

"What about it then? Five bucks?"

We had reached the spit of open land the city was in the process of reclaiming and which narrowed the waters between our grass-covered parkland and the tall highrises of the West End opposite. A man was laughingly chasing his small son and a Chinese youth flew his kite even higher than the buildings across the choppy stretch of water.

"If you're willing to swear you'll return to the Ritz and tell Peter you're sorry and are prepared to start work right away."

He seemed to be aware that he was in the fresh air, in the wash of warm sunshine, for the first time since leaving the dank apartment. He stopped, stretched out his arms and breathed in. "Nice breeze off the sea," he said. "Don't need my jacket on."

I offered to hold it. He ignored that and taking it off, draped it over his arm. He was more than just a slim figure standing there in his shirtsleeves. You could've called him downright emaciated. But his biceps stood out, and so did the muscles about his uncluttered throat. He turned fully towards me, his back now to the sun-sparkling blue of English Bay.

"Could you make that a sawbuck?"

My ignorance was genuine. "What's that?"

"Ten small ones, my friend. I need new underwear. I'm not wearing any under these jeans."

I took out my wallet, but the whole action was slowed by instinctive reluctance. Cornish canniness churned in me but I fought it back. He watched me carefully as I pulled out the bills from their compartment. I experienced a sense of relief when I found I had no fives: only a ten, a twenty, and a single dollar bill. I quickly pushed the twenty back out of sight and extracted the ten.

"You're lucky," I said, "I don't have anything else." I saw that he was still watching my wallet and suspected he thought I was lying. "That I could possibly let you have," I added.

He took the money, folded it and stuck it in the pocket of his denim shirt. I was rather shocked at the casualness of the gesture. "Don't lose it," I warned. "There's no more where that came from." He had already started quickening his pace and once more I had to make an effort to draw abreast. When I did he had another request for me.

"Davey, remember what you said about Ken? About what you told him?"

"I remember very well," I said slowly.

"Will you promise not to tell him any more? Like about today, for instance?"

It was my turn to be disingenuous. "What kind of things do you mean?"

He grinned impishly. Now he wore insouciance like an armour — so that he seemed invulnerable to embarassment. "That we kinda shouted at one another back in there. Disagreed and that? And that you loaned me the sawbuck. I don't want him thinking you give me bread 'cos it's just this one loan, see. I don't ever want anything more off you."

I looked him straight in the eyes as I lied. "I won't mention it if you don't want me to. It's just something between the two of us — how's that?"

He smiled happily, swinging his arm, as if pitching in baseball. "I knew you'd understand, Pal. Say! Let's go down the beach and skim stones, eh? Like I was the champ back home." He shouted gaily into the wind off the water. "I was the skimmer king of the Ottawa Valley — I was the ace of Carleton Place!"

We went down to the sand and the sea's frothy edge. My top effort was a three — with a flat piece of slate. Fred got a six — with a less smooth pebble. Once more I was aware of those muscled arms of his and the power of them. When he threw sometimes the small stone disappeared from my sight long before it had dropped to the sea's surface for the last time. I became both bored and fatigued long before he apparently was, and was relieved when he eventually suggested he had had enough and wanted to return home.

Just before we had retraced our steps through the last stand of trees he suddenly told me how much he had enjoyed our expedition to the beach. He also told me how he preferred the westcoast to Ontario and was glad he'd come to Vancouver. He found my hand and squeezed it.

I did not accompany him indoors this time but got into the Peugeot as he bounced towards his garden entrance to the apartment, like a happy teenager. I had switched on the ignition but not put the car into gear as I waited for him to vanish from sight. Then he turned and looked towards me. I waved goodbye but he didn't return the gesture. I guess he had looked around because he was wondering why I hadn't yet driven off.

I had a weird feeling after I did pull away from the curb. Not so much a feeling as vague sensation. When Ken got home I told him everything that had happened — although, come to think of it, I did omit mention of the ten dollar loan. The next morning we went shopping for a dinner party we were giving and the trip took us to our favorite bakery which was on the way to Kits Point. It was Ken who actually suggested we drop by and see if Fred had left for the Ritz yet. I was afraid to.

The rest is anti-climax, as they say. Long before we walked up the narrow path I knew what we were going to encounter. Fred had left the telephone that Ken had rented for him and the furniture we had accumulated at auction and from friends. That was about all, though. Of his own possessions there was no trace. Gone, too, was the radio and small cassette player I had lent him. Even the cut-glass vase which had held the mock orange was no more; the white flowers on the floor.

6

WHEN THE FATHERS WENT AWAY

I first encountered Joanna MacDonald on the University of British Columbia campus — though she quickly informed me that she was not a student. I reciprocated by admitting I wasn't faculty either. It was an early afternoon in May and as I stood by the flagpole, looking in the direction of Howe Sound, I was vaguely aware of a few early blossoms in the rose garden below me; much more conscious of the continuing brilliance of azaleas and rhododendrons in the shrubbery to the east.

She was short and had black hair cut in a boyish fringe across her forehead. There was little else remarkable — until she addressed me in a really deep contralto voice. "Days like this aren't supposed to happen. The atmosphere's too clear for May. At least that's what they told me before I came west."

"Let's keep it a secret, then. I won't tell 'em if you promise you won't."

She laughed and I warmed to her ease with a greying stranger. "I love secrets, even if I am lousy at keeping them," she said. "Say, what do you do? I'm a poet."

"Can you prove it?" I deliberately avoided mention of my own activities.

To my surprise, and also that of an elderly couple who had left their Oldsmobile with its yellow Alberta plates to appreciate the westcoast spring blossoms, Joanna began to recite. It was a strange, old-fashioned poem in regular metre and clothed in dreadfully stale images. The subject matter was a young girl hooked on heroin and living a bleak life on the street. Now this was the mid 1970s and the psychedelic days were over. Kids weren't o.d.ing as part of the diurnal mosaic any more. The talk was no longer of 'smack', 'horse', and 'Acapulco Gold'. The 'onkhs' had been laid to rest in drawers and barbers were solvent again.

But it wasn't nostalgia which bent my ear to the succession of romantic stanzas: it was the vulnerability behind her impoverished vocabulary. The didactic side of me stirred restlessly — only to subside in something approaching awe in the presence of this reckless young girl peeling away her protections.

When she had finished her recitation the Albertan with his stetson and his blue-rinsed wife, smirked their embarrassment and hurried down the rose-garden steps. That left just the two of us.

"Is the poem about you?" I asked.

"In a sort of way, I guess. I mean I've never been strung out on H but I know the girl the poem's about. I hang around The Cecil and The Blackstone. Like I know the scene?"

She looked to me as if the only scene she knew was one with big, golden teddy bears, warm flannel pyjamas, ponies and bicycles — and perhaps a bucket and spade on a tide-departed beach. Then I realised I was furnishing her with the paraphernalia of my own childhood in a distant Cornwall which seemed even more distant in time.

"You sure are staring! I didn't mean to get you uptight. It's only a poem, Man!" The glance of interrogation had switched to lip-trembling anxiety. I told myself I'd rarely met anyone whose facial expressions changed so swiftly and sharply. I was reminded of clouds flitting across an empty sky. It was suddenly important to reassure her.

"Forgive me. Your poem just set something off in me."

"Well I'm sure glad of that. Say, you tired of counting sails out there? Let's go have a coffee by the bookstore."

I wasn't really in the mood for that watery crud in styrofoam cups — nor for the incessant sound of student chatter and even louder laughter. "I've got a better idea. How about me driving us down to Spanish Banks and a walk along the beach?"

I think she decided then on a second evaluation of me. "You're not a weirdo, are you? You're not into rape or that stuff?"

I asured her that I wasn't and even went as far as to hint that I lived with a roommate. I thought she glanced at the grey hairs about my temples but that may have been my self-consciousness at alluding to Ken's existence. In any event she followed me docilely enough to the car in the Faculty Club parking lot where it sat — courtesy of Ken's sticker.

On the way down the winding road, in the shadow of the forested cliff, my new acquaintance said very little. I gathered she was absorbing our Peugeot 404 which happened to be new. She made a couple of comments about foreign cars, utilized the cigarette lighter on the dash, pulled out the ashtray and switching on the radio, quickly turned the knob from CBC-FM (where Ken and I permanently left it) and made for the AM band and a local rock station. That didn't please me as I wanted to admire her taste as much as I admired her pert little face, but the drive was too short for me to contemplate re-asserting my captaincy of the car and returning the radio to the scratchy recording of Claudia Muzio that classical DJ Bob Kerr was playing from his own collection.

Just before I turned off the road for the beach carpark she culturally redeemed herself in my anti-populist eyes. She noticed a copy of Audrey Thomas' *Munchmeyer & Prospero and the Island* on the glove shelf. "You like her stuff?" she asked. "I read *Mrs. Blood.* She's great don't you think?"

I told her enthusiastically that I agreed as I pulled up and switched off the ignition and the rock music. I warmed for a good chat about the novels and stories of Audrey Thomas but the anticipation was short-lived. My comely young pasenger was already out of the car, waving her arms in the direction of the lighthouse at Point Atkinson and dancing wildly about as if auditioning for Anna Wyman's Dance Troupe. I had to break into a trot to catch up with her.

Just as I reached her she veered off in the direction of the city. If ever Vancouver looked like a coastal Trebizond in the golden sunlight it was at that moment.

"A man once told me," I began, "that when he came to live here, just before World War Two, there wasn't a light to be seen at night over there on the north shore. For one thing it was mainly just summer homes. 'Camps' I think he called them. That was the term around here — not cabins."

She didn't reply but abruptly stopped her prancing on the flat wet sand and looked at me. Little oyster catchers ran jerkily towards the fret of the receding tide. There was just time to hear their piping before her plaint sounded on the breeze that led from her to me. "Must be nice to remember things like that. I've not got anything to remember, really."

"Youth certainly has its compensations," I said. Then tried to redeem myself before she realised how smug I could be. "The likes of me would cheerfully surrender every tacky memory to be able to skip and jump like you can. You make beautiful movements, do you know that?"

That started her off on another tack. "Look at this, then," she shouted. And started to cartwheel her slim, blue-jeaned form across the smooth beach. This evoked an extraordinary sensation in me. Not lust exactly. Indeed, no erotic gratification whatever. After all, I have known this particular body's appetites for forty or so years and the sight of a trim young girl — however boyish her contours — wasn't calculated to feed any of them! Nevertheless I was profoundly moved by that energetic form which succumbed so lightly to the chains of gravity as she abruptly switched to somersaults and from that to open-arm, open-legged, leaps towards the silvered heat of the sun.

I glanced quickly about me. The beach was vacant. I asked myself if *that* mattered... Joanna didn't allow of further introspection. Suddenly the acrobatics were over, her arm thrust through the crook of mine, and she was begging me to identify the various seabirds that either ran like mice ahead of us or took noisily to the air in small groups.

All enthusiasm, I launched into descriptions. "Those are turnstones. They usually fly in flocks like that and their sound is *very* characteristic. Those over there are sandpipers and mergansers — while bobbing in the water closest to you? Those really pretty ducks with the white patches and orange head stripes? They're harlequins..." I suddenly broke off, embarrassed by my own pedantry.

She didn't seem to notice. Instead kept nodding sagely as she looked carefully from one cluster of shorebirds to another.

"Why?" I asked tentatively, "why did you think I'd know which bird was what?"

Again that odd look, as if she were absorbing my every word. "I knew you would. It's your vibes. I just knew you'd know all about such things."

"I'd better stop while I'm ahead," I told her. "Any moment you're going to discover the truth about grey-headed strangers and I'm not sure you're ready for it. It isn't like those fatherly lawyers on television who seem to have all the answers."

"I don't watch TV any more," she advised me brightly. "I did as a kid but now I'm more interested in learning about the environment. Eco-systems, that kind of jazz. In other words all this." The circular movement of her outstretched arm generously included the snow-capped northshore mountains, the dark smear of coniferous Stanley Park and the waters of English Bay as well as the sunlit buildings of the West End. I smiled at the sheer extravagance of her gesture — but kept the thought to myself.

As we walked along the foreshore and she began to emote in all directions as if deprived of a main verb to hold her sense together, I decided it was time to glean some rather more concrete information from this lively young lady. Enough of these disconnected eulogies for the twin peaks of the Lions and the mysterious advance on the city by an encroaching Mount Baker as it kept creeping closer to the Canadian border.

I wanted respite from all these wild songs for Vancouver and more, much more, about her. I didn't bargain for her steely determination.

"Do you live all alone?" I asked.

The reply was a prompt affirmation but she switched the questioning to me — and in an approximate area. "You say you have a roommate — is he much younger than you?"

"A little younger," I told her reluctantly. "Now how about an expresso bar? I know a good one."

The subsequent visit to the teen-age haunt on Fourth Avenue was not a success. She seemed restless amid her peers who noisily crowded the place, and kept darting me glances which I found unsettling. "Why keep looking at me like that? Do I stand out as such a sore thumb?" I couldn't hide my petulance.

She swilled her cappucino in its transparent cup, rattled the saucer beneath. "I guess I don't go too much for this joint. Kinda square, don't you think?"

I made no effort to reply.

"So the middle classes of Point Grey don't turn me on," she persisted.

"You have an excellent eye for social nuance," I suggested coldly. "I personally couldn't tell whether these kids were from ritzy Shaughnessy or shitty East Hastings."

She pouted. "Why should you? To you they're all just kids, anyway."

I stood up to leave. One or two of the lads were languishing looks in her direction and I had the uncomfortable notion that if she responded to their little stallion gestures and comments her language would have been succinct and *not* very nice.

We were headed downtown before I asked her where she wanted to be dropped off.

"Anyplace," she said vaguely. "When we going to meet again? And where?"

It was at that moment I realised I had already assumed a further meeting. Also that I didn't want a long period to elapse before that happened. "What about tomorrow afternoon?" she suggested. "By the railings above the open-air stage of the Kits Showboat? If it's raining there's a shelter right next to the concession."

"That a favorite stamping ground of yours?" I asked mischievously. "You've gotten the details down so pat it sounds as if you always meet your pick-ups there."

Her expression darkened immediately and she was all fiery hostility. "What an asshole thing to say! Know what you are? A prick. Now let me out of here." She started fumbling with the door and I had a flush of fear that she would pitch herself out into the flowing traffic. As if from a place apart, somewhere outside myself, I heard myself pleading forgiveness, apologising for at least the second time since I'd met her for some unwonted turn of speech at which she'd taken instant offence. But she seemed to be mollified as quickly as I told her I was sorry for my stupidity. The contracted brow and tight mouth turned suddenly to a demure smile. "I guess we're both different from what we're used to. It'll get easier as time goes on. You'll see. Better drop me at the next light. Don't forget about tomorrow. Don't go standing me up, o.k.?"

I was still eagerly reassuring her as I let her get out at Fourth and Burrard and would have gone on doing so, had she not started at once walking briskly towards the bridge and downtown.

An odd thing happened when Ken got home that evening and asked what I had been writing that afternoon and if there was anything for me to read aloud to him over drinks. I began truthfully enough by reminding him that it had been the day reserved for a visit to the University library, for me to check a number of facts pertaining to my biography of Vancouver's turn-of-the-century mayor, David Oppenheimer. But at that juncture — to my own mounting incredulity — deviousness took over.

I did not exactly *lie* but I took meticulous care not to tell the truth. I said I'd taken a long stroll along the beach — but I made no reference at all to Joanna MacDonald. As Ken gently stirred a second swatch of gibson martinis the tinkling of ice in the pitcher proved a delicious diversion to my ears and I think he was mildly taken aback when I launched into an abruptly invented hymn to the familiar sound — likening it to some bars from Schubert's *Trout Quintet*.

Conversation turned to general music matters after that and when I left our small house behind its giant screen of laurel the next afternoon, ostensibly to visit a female descendant of Vancouver's only Jewish mayor, I was sorely aware that it was still with Joanna's identity carefully concealed from my roommate of twenty years. In fact not until I saw her lolling there by the railings did the full weight of deception lift. If anything, she looked more fetching than on the previous day. Her mouth crinkled charmingly upwards as she watched my coming and she was screaming greetings to me long before I was in earshot. An old man in an over-sized cloth cap (which would have suited her delightfully which is why I can still recall him) shook his head in dissension to whatever she was calling out, then shuffled off in the direction of the row of white-coned chestnuts that formed an *allée* thus splitting the grass areas bordering the actual beach.

We walked towards the old CPR locomotive which still stood there in those days and on which children loved to play. Joanna was talking incessantly if vaguely then abruptly zeroed in on me.

"You were right on time! Heh! I've never known anyone into that punctuality bit. Most people think nothing of standing you up for an hour or so." Her praise inspired both my grin and my sudden putting of my arm about her shoulders. "I've thought a lot about you since yesterday afternoon — wondering whether you were with your pals in The Castle or The Blackstone."

She corrected me quickly. "Blackstone or *The Cecil*."

She didn't elaborate and I certainly wasn't going to ask whether it was that all-boy element in The Castle which had occasioned her contradiction. Instead I changed the subject as we came alongside the historic locomotive which had one small child sitting astride its smokestack. "There's a lad who's going to be an engineer when he grows up," I remarked.

But she had already clambered up to the cab and climbed along the black-painted water tank towards the youngster perched in front of her. She shouted for me to join her but I smilingly refused. I was fully prepared to yield to her sparkle, but not to the point of making myself ridiculous. However, after a glance about the macadam'd area to make sure I was unobserved, I compromised to the extent of standing self-consciously on the footplate. That was where she found me when she eventually climbed down. I was swinging my left foot nonchalantly — rather regretting I had put on my best black loafers before leaving the house. But in Joanna's presence there was little time for such minor considerations. She was already suggesting we walk around the bluff to the marina under Burrard Bridge. If we walked in that direction, she said, she'd reward me by revealing her favorite secret place. I felt incapable of refusing her. Instead I mentally put on hold my interview with the Oppenheimer descendant for another and Joanna-less day.

Her private hideout proved to be at the foot of a knoll within the small region of scrub, mainly alder, near the stanchions of the bridge. I knew it well. It was, and is, a rather unfrequented area where hassled dog-owners take their charges for exercise and where, in late summer, knowing blackberry pickers congregate for an ample harvest amid the profusion of bramble bushes.

Walking single-file along the tortuous path that snaked through those bushes, I learned a few more things about Joanna MacDonald. She had recently broken with her boyfriend — indeed 'recent' would have applied to the time frame in which she despatched her past *three* boyfriends! Even her voyage to the westcoast had really been occasioned by the termination of an affair and since then, in quick succession, she'd moved out of the pad of a Simon Fraser University drop-out named Mike; and split after a brief spell in a West End highrise from a clerk called Alistair, who shared an apartment with a previous girlfriend and a boy named Bruce from Nanaimo. The nature of Alistair's relationship with Bruce had only subsequently become manifest to Joanna.

"That's what I couldn't hack," she explained on the way back to the car. "Jesus! I don't care what the guy does — but he's gotta level. Don't you agree?"

I agreed.

From that breathless account of a short-lived *ménage à quatre* on the twenty-second floor of a West End apartment she broke off sharply to offer the information that while living ostensibly with Alistair she had contracted some kind of vaginal fungus. It was my turn to abruptly change the subject.

"Tell me about Master Alistair. What made you suspect you had rivals of all genders?" I wasn't particularly proud of my prudishness on hearing the fungoid price tag of her sexual profligacy spelled out, but I was old enough to know that I had to work within my own limitations. One such limitation was an acute distaste over the kind of thing this liberated young woman seemed able to mention without any palpable cost!

Joanna seemed, however, to be not at all interested in Alistair, Bruce, Michael and the unnamed predecessor from Toronto, now they belonged to her past. Her very next sentence sustantiated the impression. "I know a great place to eat. It's called Wong Ho's and it does the best Dim Sum in town."

I could call to mind at least three places — even in those very early days of Dim Sum popularity in Vancouver — which had a better range of dishes and better prepared, too, than Wong Ho's but decided to mention none of them. "I'd thought of taking you to a little Portuguese restaurant off Commercial. The fish is fresh every day and..."

"Sure! Sure! I'd rather go to some favorite place of yours for this first time. Restaurants can tell you a lot about a guy. Mike liked all the White Spots and Alistair, for Chrissakes, always hung around that Denny's on Broadway and wouldn't even eat Chinese with me. Only Bruce would do that — and then just to spite Alistair."

The lunch itself turned out to be a great success with Joanna quickly endearing her nubile self to Alberto Queiroz, the bachelor brother of the owner, Carlos-Maria. Sitting opposite me seemed to stir her flirtatiousness. But if she batted dark eyebrows for the attentive young Portuguese charmer, I was convinced that she rolled those grey eyes for me alone. Every now and then she would grab my hand across the snow white tablecloth, clasp it within hers and, from beneath her chair, find my foot with her sneakers and apply pressure. It was in truth a delightful meal, which left me so bemused that I didn't hesitate to agree to attend Wong Ho's with her and affect delight in their indifferent Dim Sum.

It was not to a restaurant, though, that she took me a couple of evenings later when Ken was teaching a night-course. It was to a light-flashing, go-go prancing warehouse space with three bars and a small, jammed, dance floor. Somehow she lured me onto it and proceeded to propel me to a spot where the noise was so deafening I couldn't distinguish between the head-achey thunder under my skull and the external taped bedlam to which the packed and squirming young were shaking their bodies.

After two or three self-conscious shimmies opposite a grinning Joanna I was panting, sweating and dying to sit down. When there finally came a lull in the cacophony and I could flee to the circumference of that sea of milling bodies (with Joanna grabbing my damp shirt from behind) it was to discover the few wall stools occupied. There was only the smallest of spaces to huddle against other hot bodies, close weary eyelids against the harsh, refracted light, and with each heavy breath drawn in the unholy stench of dust and sweat. In all my life I had never felt more out of place and — staring down at Joanna's flushed and excited face — more ancient and decrepit.

It took me two days and the mystified glances of a patently curious Ken, to recover. And if I never informed him of the real reason for aching muscles and painful back, nor did I let on to Joanna how much I loathed her dancing spot. I persuaded her for our next meeting that we rendezvous in the cocktail bar of the Georgia Hotel. I grudgingly accepted the fact that her youthful soul might find the place duller and staider than The Gandy Dancer, but at least I was less likely to risk a heart seizure.

I ordered a gibson. She had a beer. She munched hungrily at the bowl of salted peanuts. I resisted them.

This is the fourth time we've met," I began. "We've never missed more than two consecutive days, do you realize."

"So what's there to realize?" Her smile was quite gone.

I looked about us in the gloom of the cocktail lounge with the air of a Corsican conspirator. "Someone will see us, my dear. The jig will be up!"

She was ready with a curt response to my mock dramatics. "Not, my dear, if if we'd gone to The Gandy Dancer instead of this businessman's pisshole! Or even The Cecil. I'm sure no-one would know you there."

Bowing to her raillery I ruefully acknowledged the truth of that but she was still disinclined to let me off the hook. "Besides, what difference would it make? So a couple of people meet by the U.B.C. flagpole and find they got a few things in common. Big deal!"

It was then this particular worm turned. "Isn't that just a little disingenuous?"

"What's *that* mean? You questioning my genius or something?"

But I wasn't going to play any more teacher-student games. "You're being obtuse — don't pretend you can't see the implications of being seen day after day with a man old enough to be your father."

"That sure seems to be a thing with you. I've never known a guy who harps so much on his age. You know what you are? A kinda Zsa Zsa Gabor in *reverse*! And what's this 'day after day' crap? Jesus, it's never more than for a couple of hours, man!"

"I've made you mad, haven't I?" I was genuinely distressed to hear that harsh cut to her voice; to see the small hands bunched tightly in her lap. She had stopped picking at the nuts.

"It's all that you're-older-than-me crap," she said slowly, her voice now pure contralto. Even in that poor light I could see her eyes had mositened.

"Joanna, I'm truly sorry. It was my stupid idea of a joke, that's all."

"Well it wasn't very funny."

"I know. It was a ham-fisted way of starting off. Let me try again, will you? Please?"

She said nothing in response so I forged ahead. "I'm getting a guilty consciece. That's what I really want to say. About the amount of time I've spent — well, goofing off. More over the past two weeks than the last two months. I have a deadline, you see. The book I'm on."

A smile finally illumined her face. "Now I know what you do! You've given yourself away! So you're a book writer — and I'm a reader. When I'm not writing my poetry, that is. That's kinda neat. We sort of complement each other."

I lifted my drink and looked across its surface at her. I was thinking that her frequently pouting mouth was as attractive as her sudden gusts of laughter and that sexy gruffness which habitually lurked about her voice. "Here's to a lot of writing and reading, then. And no more stupid questions," I toasted.

We clinked glasses. At the back of my mind, though, stubbornly remained the reason I had suggested that particular bar with its decibel rate low enough for us to talk seriously.

"That book I'm working on, Joanna? I've reached the point where I have to go out of town fairly soon. Some interviews and some more library research."

"Where you gotta go?" Never had I heard her voice pitched so low.

"San Francisco for one thing."

She took an unladylike gulp of her beer. "Lucky you!"

"It won't be quite yet. I've still got a section to finish first."

"Don't worry. I get the message."

"There is no *message*, Joanna. It is just the way I happen to work on a project like this. I have to stick to schedules — handle my time properly."

"Time — slime," she sang tunelessly. "And it all boils down to 'Joanna, don't interfere with my life and fuck up my schedule'."

"Now you're just being silly," I said, tight-lipped.

"That's just the point. I *am* silly. I was hoping that being around Davey Bryant would make me less so. No crime in that, is there?"

"No, I take it back. You're not silly. In fact you've got a lot on the ball.

I'd always give you A's for answers, Joanna, even if I might fail you for your logic in arriving at them."

"Don't *patronise* me, for Chrissakes! I want none of that 'There, there little girl — here's a pat on the head for being a good kid and knowing when to butt out'."

We were getting nowhere, I decided. "If you'll finish up your beer I'll drive you home. We're not getting anywhere tonight." She didn't answer but swirled the remnants of her Molson's around her glass.

"And we must arrange our next meeting," I continued. "Perhaps over the weekend we could take a hike in the University Endowment Lands. The trails are beautiful this time of year."

"You can't drive me home," she said with deliberation, "because I'm already here. Like I told you, man. I'm a street person. What I didn't tell you is that I know half the hotels in downtown Vancouver. Sometimes I end up in one of 'em on my own — sometimes not on my own. I have a sort of moveable pad, get it?"

I stared at her, wondering whether she was having me on. Now I felt quite unable to read her face: certainly not those large grey eyes that stared back so unflinchingly into mine. I decided to use bluff.

"None of us are saints. Besides, I can see you thrive on fresh experience. And at your age, why shouldn't you? If anything I envy you."

It was immediately evident that such was not the reply Joanna sought. "I didn't say I *liked* what happened. Matter of fact I hate waking up next to a strange head on the goddamn pillow."

I grimaced. "You certainly make it sound unpleasant — but presumably by the next morning you're more familiar with each other than when you met?"

The young dislike sarcasm. Joanna hated it. "When you talk like that it makes me think you must cheat a lot on that guy you live with."

Imprudently I fled yet again to the armour of sarcasm. "You're a born psychiatrist, do you know that? You can obviously read me like one of those books you tell me you're always reading. When not writing poetry, that is."

Fortunately there was only a little beer left at the bottom of her glass for what there was she suddenly threw into my startled face. Then she began to cry. There was an unpleasantly longish interval when I grew warm with the realization that the waiters and the other customers instinctively knew that this was no father and daughter matter. I finally managed to pay the bill, bring down her energetic upset from noisy crying to intermittent sobs, and steer her successfully past the crowded tables and to the night air and the relief of the hotel carpark.

She let me drive her two or three blocks, then signalled for me to pull over. We were still in the hotel and office block area. I was convinced she didn't live in that vicinity, in spite of her story. But I offered no questions and she volunteered no information. For a few minutes we sat there motionless, bathed in the feeble light of a street lamp. It was one of those rare moments when I was aware of the car clock ticking.

"You don't really want to see me again, do you?" she said eventually.

How explain to her that I did? Terribly. Only that I was *frightened*. And not only for her but for me, too? That the older you get, the more desperate. That the small risks of youth take on the cutting edge of a razor blade when the patterns of life have become more brittle: the emotions then more likely to break than bend... She risked vaginal fungus and God-knows what else, just for everyday lust. I was fearful and agitated at the tiniest throb of sexual attraction which she managed to spark in middle-aged, gay me. So I didn't answer her directly. Instead I sat there making lightning calculations over the future — balancing the celibately safe against the erotically unknown; the visibly snug against the teeth of the dark.

I sighed finally, from a profoundly disturbed depth. "Perhaps we should step back and look at things more coolly. Things have been so hectic between us."

"Meaning don't bother to call us — we'll call you?"

That was easier to deal with. "Hardly. You've never given me a number, Joanna. And do you know how many J. MacDonalds there are in the Vancouver phone book?"

"Can I help it if I don't have a goddamned telephone? Why can't I call you?"

"You can. Around 6 p.m. is a good time. And not too much after 7 p.m. as we go out quite a bit. The weekends aren't too good either. We usually take the receiver off if we're entertaining. And we go to bed fairly early so I wouldn't try after 11 p.m."

To all that she nodded slowly, as if absorbing each detail, piecemeal. Then she abruptly stiffened. "Good. I gotta go." And with a violent, circular movement, she grabbed her tote bag, pulled her coat about her, and fled the car, I watched her lope down the street. She didn't turn back to wave farewell.

When she did phone it was almost two months later! Just before midnight when we had both put our books down, ensured the dogs had settled, and switched off both bedside lights. The closest phone was in my study and I volunteered to answer it. At first, I must confess, I hadn't a clue as to the caller. If it hadn't been the voice of a woman my surliness at that hour would have been distinctly more in evidence, but it crossed my mind that it might be one of Ken's students. As it was she sudenly asked if I was uptight because of the hour. It was then I recognized Joanna.

"What on earth happened to you? Of course I don't mind the time. I didn't only go to San Francisco, by the way, but to London and Germany, too."

"I've been over on Galiano Island," she told me in reply. "I go there quite often. You should come and see Montague Harbor, Davey. There's a swell beach there. All crushed white shells. And a pair of kingfishers and..."

I glanced at the luminous digital on my desk. "Joanna, it's past midnight. Couldn't we talk kingfishers tomorrow?"

She was quite unabashed. "Yeah, well that's why I called. If we could meet tomorrow I'll take a later ferry back to Galiano."

As she talked I paged through my engagement diary. "How about lunch? One o'clock at The Beach Café at the foot of Denman? Can you manage that?"

"Of course we can manage that!" she mimicked my voice in response. Then clicked the receiver down. Just before I drifted off to sleep it occurred to me that she had used 'we' rather than 'I' in terms of the proposed lunch, and I wondered uneasily what she had meant.

I was not left long in doubt when I parked behind the restaurant and saw her standing on the sidewalk across the road from the beach at English Bay. Next to her, with the seersucker jacket of his suit draped over his shoulder revealing a cream shirt and orange silk tie, was a gent of my own vintage. His profuse gray curls on his bared head danced merrily in the breeze from the sea on that blithe summer's day. Quite simply, for me it was dislike at first sight! Looking down quickly at his paunch I knew immediately how tight he had notched his belt. I also sensed that the top button of his shirt was pressing cruelly into the ample flesh of his throat. I rarely wore ties any more for that very reason...

On a sickly sea of false *bonhomie* I learned his name was Colin, that he was a realtor in suburban Richmond, and that he was precisely one year younger than I. When we had climbed upstairs to the restaurant's second floor and a panting Colin had excused himself to visit the washroom I forced my own breath to come regularly as I listened to a radiant Joanna telling me that they had met some three weeks before on Galiano where he had a cabin halfway up-island and that they were copulating with the intensity and frequency of rabbits. She also breezily informed me that he was twenty-three years married and that his wife and two daughters — both older than Joanna — lived with him. They were as unaware of Joanna's existence as they were of the Galiano love-nest. The man had even had the gall to tell Joanna that there had been a string of young women like her in his life and that none of them had ever made contact with his suburban-based situation.

By this time her philandering suitor was about to rejoin us and I was so agitated by her blissfully delivered information that I not only had difficulty in reading the absurdly large menu — I could hardly hold it. The lunch, for me, was a total disaster. Only years of gay discretion in public places prevented me rising abruptly, informing me how ridiculous was their conduct opposite me, and blundering wildly out of the restaurant. But by their simpering exchanges and moony expressions, the grotesquely ill-suited pair proved they were quite oblivious to my distress.

Not even when I finally blurted my goodbyes and had left the table before they were ready, did they seem even faintly aware that I was put out. When I took a last scowl at them through the bannisters before descending the steep stairs, it was to observe them still smiling into each other's eyes as his ugly old hand reached out across the damask tablecloth to squeeze her fingers.

7

DAVEY'S DREAM
or
THE RELUCTANT CLUB

Parents for me have always made poor fiction, so that I have often resorted to adoptions such as uncles and aunts, family friends and even enemies, to make the multiple grafts to turn into a Mum or a Dad. But sometimes I have turned to my friends and borrowed their fathers and mothers for my devious purposes. For the occasion I have in mind, the acquiring of Hubert's mother was compounded by her image filtering through a provisional succession of dreams.

I have never met Mrs. Hewlett-Whyte save through a couple of long letters that eventually reached her portly, middle-aged son with the fruity British accent and an impoverished mode of living as a part-time assistant in a sleazy art gallery (European Oils at Discount!) on South Granville Street. But I visualized her quite clearly by the second time we met old Hubert when he was walking his pug, Cristobel, at Jericho Beach where we daily take our two dogs. He talked of her incessantly and still does, though the time of our first meeting occurred back in the early 1970s.

I first dreamed of her, I suppose, as Hubert's mother, then as some kind of ancient aunt of mine, and finally as my own mother — where she lodged in my nightime skull for some considerable time. Now, however, some ten years later, she has faded from my dreamworld and has reverted to mothering poor Hubert who has become quite ill and talks a lot about her as he lies so wan and deflated in St. Paul's Hospital.

But in 1979 she was the distinct if ethereal property — by pseudo filial connection — of Davey Bryant, and it is on the strength of that I can tell you all about The Reluctant Club, my imagined mother and her friend, and the seedy district of North London where that club was evoked.

* * *

Mrs. Daphne Hewlett-Whyte, to give her the name of her third and final husband, peered out of the grimy, barred window of her Islington flat, and addressed the plump thrush enjoying the spring sun.

"Well, birdie, darling. Do you think Mumsie will enjoy it as much as you?"

As if in answer the bird fluffed up its feathers and emitted a stream of crystal-clear song. It did Mrs. Hewlett-Whyte's heart good, she told herself, pulling her angora beret over her reddish-dyed hair. All the same, it was only March and there was that daffy rhyme about the clout business, which she couldn't quite recollect. So she put a second cardigan on under her heavy tweed coat, and then eyed her handiwork at the mirror next to the window facing the area steps of Number 43, Ainsley Road.

Behind her the clock on the crowded mantelpiece informed her it was nine o'clock, after its Westminster chimes prelude, and she realized she was a little later than usual that morning. She rubbed one shoe against the thickness of her lisle stocking on the other leg, and smiled in recognition of the sense of girlish naughtiness which overcame her whenever she so lazily effected a shine to her footwear.

But the smile in the mirror was shortlived. Not merely because Daphne Hewlett-Whyte was sorely conscious of the artificial disappearance of grey hair, of the mass of wrinkles that disfigured her once beautiful face, but because she was painfully aware that seventy-odd years stood between her standing there and the time she could be truly described as a little girl.

Her sigh as she turned away, was quite audible. It took so little to plummet Daphne's mood from high elation to the abyss of despair in this graceless year of 1979 which had seen her eighty-first birthday pass, virtually unobserved.

Outside she wrapped her rather scruffy fur-piece close about her neck. The March morning was less clement than that foolish thrush had suggested, she reflected ruefully, then concluded that perhaps the bird had been singing so energetically just to keep warm! The conceit amused her and she felt immediately better. To sustain the sense of wellbeing as she trudged down the unrelievedly grey street which was narrow enough to funnel a cold wind conveying particles of grit that smacked unpleasantly against her old flesh, she turned her thoughts to the sweet consolations of the remote past.

Across the street, holding the loose leash of an orange pomeranian which was in the act of peeing against a lamp post, was a woman who lived two floors above Daphne. Mrs. Hewlett-Whyte had always felt she was a coarse creature and was irritated by her patronizing way of invariably addressing the basement tenant as 'luv' or 'dearie'.

Daphne tossed her head and walked a little more quickly. What would a common creature like Mrs. Stokes, middle-aged widow of a publican, know about those madcap days in London during the 'Twenties, when Daphne had been the intimate of such literary luminaries as D.H. Lawrence, Aldous Huxley and Bunny Garnet? What indeed would any of these Ainsley Road crowd she now knew and with whom she forced herself to exchange pleasantries, have in common with her erstwhile friends of Holland Park and Chelsea, of the Riviera in the 'Twenties and 'Thirties, who wrote books and plays, designed ballets and dined riotously at the Café Royal?

Mrs. Hewlett-Whyte shook the carefully reddened curls which peeked from under the white beret. What a rich past had been hers! What friends and lovers! What parties! She slowed her pace again as her mind's eye lived once more those idyllic, smiling scenes, invariably enacted in sunlight, which corresponded to the sepia'd snapshots carefully mounted in the album in the top drawer of her dressing table.

This way the hurt of the present was anaelsiad by the balm of the past, so that the aggression of those bleak streets through which she wended on her way to the shops, was withdrawn. Mrs. Stokes, Johnson, the butcher to whose store Daphne was currently heading, saw only this tarted-up old lady with an extravagant Edwardian accent, but she knew herself to be the onetime lover of England's most famous poet and the mother of a leading man of letters, as her offspring had been inclined to describe himself.

Not that for one moment did Mrs. Hewlett-Whyte reject such a title for her son, Hubert. Indeed, she was convinced that his was a major literary talent and that his picture books were brilliantly evocative; his memoirs vivid. All this in spite of the great hurt he had inflicted upon her by departing so precipitately for Canada five years previously, and for not having corresponded frequently with her since surfacing in Vancouver.

When Daphne arrived outside the butcher's, she decided to go first to the Christian Science Reading Room for a little sit-down. Thoughts of the errant Hubert invariably depleted her. Besides, the buffeting wind had tired her more than she was accustomed to on that daily progress from her flat to the shops and she knew that the people at the Reading Room did not frown too much when elderly folk like herself availed themselves of Christian Science chairs.

She adjusted her beret mechanically from years of practice, for the Christian Science premises understandably offered no mirror. Once she was ensconced, her mind drifted back to her son again from whom she hadn't even received a Christmas card in 1978, although there had been a brief note on her birthday. But she wasn't thinking of his failure to write but of the priceless carpets which had adorned the floors of her flat with yet another worn and venerable from Persia, hung upon the wall. This had not been simply an echo of Hubert's interior decorator days — he had done so *many* things, she sighed — but also served to obscure the unsightly collection of pipes that ran across the basement wall. But the carpets, along with the cloisonné vase, that some man with a lisp, she remembered, had given Hubert years ago, had long since gone. That is taken by Hubert before his departure to Canada, and sold to an avid buyer whom he'd met at Sotheby's, he informed her, and who had taken such a shine to Hubert and his erudite taste, that her son had been periodically invited down to some vast mansion near Horsham.

There was little left in the flat as mementoes of Hubert's more spacious days, for the last vestiges of them had been removed by him, even as she had stood there tearfully protesting his action. He had sought to reason with her; emphasizing over and over again that these postwar times were especially hard for artists like him, and that the people he had to deal with all the time were savage and uncouth. He reminded her of the comment that Norman Douglas had made when Hubert was a mere youth, visiting the famous author on Capri. Referring to critics and publishers in particular, Douglas had said. "They eat you raw, my dear. They eat you raw!"

She must have said the words aloud, while sitting there in the Reading Room, for Mrs. Hewlett-Whyte was suddenly aware that she had attracted the frowning attention of the plain little woman who managed the place. She was feeling in no mood to explain Norman Douglas to an inferior so reluctantly got to her feet again.

Daphne then decided to go to the post office, collect her pension, and purchase an airletter form to write yet again to Hubert and explain about the cost of living and how difficult it was for her to eke out her widow's and old age pension which were currently her sole source of income.

She spun the post-office business out by leaving the first queue she joined when midway to the counter, and then tacking onto the back of a longer one. Her excuse for this odd behavior was the sight of an old friend in the second line-up. But when she arrived it was to discover that it was not Gertie Madison-Lynch standing there. Indeed, close up, this woman did not look even vaguely like Gertie...

When she finally left the post office she saw by the clock in its window that it was nearly ten o'clock. There was nothing left to do now but go to the butcher's for the small piece of liver she decided would suit her for lunch. That purchased, it would mean, of course, that she would be back in the flat with the best part of two hours to wait before frying up her meal on the hot plate. But there had been other days when she had misjudged the time and had suffered a good three hours before the distraction of luncheon itself as a relief from all that silent boredom.

There were not many fellow-customers in the butcher's: two young 'Mums' wih their off-spring strapped into push-chairs, and an elderly woman wearing an old-fashioned toque which made her look a bit like Queen Mary, Daphne thought. Indeed, on inspection the woman looked even more like the old dowager queen. The discovery pleased Mrs. Hewlett-Whyte. Somehow it compensated for the foolishness over the imagined Gertie in the post office....

Daphne would have liked to speak to this woman who seemed socially superior to the usual run of customers in Johnson's, but she was reluctant to start conversation lest she be found wrong in her social sizing-up and the wearer of the toque proved to be as vulgar and tiresome as that Mrs. Stokes and her messy little dog, from upstairs.

With the two Cockney mothers served, it was now the toque's turn. Mr. Johnson tipped his straw boater and vouchsafed her the same soppy smile beneath his ridiculously thin moustache that he bestowed upon all the Old Age Pensioners, Daphne observed coldly, regardless of their background and demeanour.

"What's it for today then, luv? Nice bit of shank?"

"Des poumons, if you please," the Toque said, in a bright, clear voice of impeccable quality — music, in fact, to Daphne's deprived ears.

"Eh? What the devil's that, then?"

"Oh, I am so dreadfully sorry! I can't think of the English term. Isn't that foolish of me!"

Mr. Johnson's smile vanished and the moustache curved scornfully. "Well, make up your mind, dear. Like there's others behind you."

At which point Mrs. Hewlett-Whyte felt it desperately incumbent upon her to unite with a woman of refinement being patronized and insulted by this *mongrel* of a shopkeeper.

"May I help?" she interjected. "We are all subject to these unfortunate lapses of memory from time to time."

The toque beamed in her direction. "Isn't it just too potty of me? It's for the cats. I've been living in Paris for over twenty years. It's meat for the cats, don't you know."

Daphne suddenly flared in understanding. "Les poumons. Of course! Lungs!" Then she turned imperiously to the obese butcher in his straw hat. "Lights, Johnson. Madame wants some lights!"

Johnson didn't bother to hide his scowl. "Why didn't she bloody well say so, then?" he muttered quite audibly before turning his back on the two ladies, to hack savagely away at some huge, pink pile — the spongey lungs of cattle.

With only the bulging nape of his neck confronting them, the two elderly women effected mutual introductions. Daphne Hewlett-Whyte thus learned that the woman from Paris bore the name of Mrs. Eleanor Elphinstone and that she was indeed the gentlewoman that her elocution had suggested. So excited was she by this discovery that Daphne broke with rigorous custom and did something entirely uncharacteristic: she asked her new acquaintance to tea that very day.

Mrs. Elphinstone, too, broke with social custom and, without even polite prevarication, answered slowly but immediately that she would like nothing better. With a rather unEnglish haste over personal revelation which Daphne was to recall later, she explained herself. "I really know nothing about this part of North London and although I read a good deal and listen to the B.B.C., I do get somewhat lonely at times."

Such bluntness of sentiment rather shocked Daphne but she warmed even more to the thin and elongated person of Mrs. Elphinstone, for her courage in speaking forth.

"I'm afraid my little place is hardly palatial," she explained carefully, before giving directions. "But it is only temporary until my son returns from abroad. And at least the bus runs right past Fortnum's and gets me even to Harrod's in an hour or so."

"I like people making friends in me shop," Johnson, the butcher, suddenly contributed. "Nice for you two to get together and have a cuppa — gets a bit lonely, don't it Mum, what with that son of yours and his little friend gone away and that."

"Good *day*, Johnson," Mrs. Hewlett-Whyte almost spat, grabbing the small package of liver from Johnson's hand dangling over the counter on which he leaned as he devoured their every exchange.

The two ladies returned glances, now both unwilling to delay in that white-tiled bleakness of the butcher's shop, with its strange feel of sawdust beneath the feet and the slightly unpleasant odor of raw meat pervading the atmosphere. Mrs. Hewlett-Whyte held the door open for her new friend and, sensing the importunate Johnson still eyeing them, parted quickly in the High Street without shaking hands. Daphne then darted into the neighboring florists for a bunch of daffodils and then hurried home to prepare for her visitor.

In the back of her mind when she let herself into the basement flat, was a decision to sit down and do what she had delayed for so long — clean the silver. But poking here and there she discovered that Hubert's frequent visits to Sotheby's over the years had depleted the family heirlooms, in this respect to so few items that a bout with the Silvo seemed hardly necessary. All that was left was a rather ugly Victorian teapot which for some reason or other had never responded to silver polish and only went blotchy, plus a couple of candlesticks which could remain on the mantelpiece where the light was poor as the tea-trolley she intended to us, certainly had no room for them on it.

One hour or so before Mrs. Elphinstone was due, Daphne surveyed the fruits of her cleaning and dusting and pronounced herself reasonably pleased. There was nothing she could do about those dreadful pipes running the length of the wall, of course; nor the constant gush and gurgle from plumbing activities above her head from the rest of the house. But the daffs looked nice on the window sill, the frayed carpet seemed a little better than usual after she had gone over it with the carpet-sweeper, and she had finally tidied up the ashes in the fireplace.

She debated whether to pull the old velvet drapes, as by teatime, she estimated, it would be dark enough to need the light on, and there was no way she could even get close to the high sash windows, let alone remove the encrusted grime from them. Her final decision was to pull them as their faded plum set off the yellow of the daffs so well. It was the kind of thing her son, Hubert, with his artistic instincts would most certainly have done, she reflected comfortably.

At three twenty-five p.m. Daphne Hewlett-Whute switched on her electric kettle to 'simmer'. But moments later she realized that was unnecessary as precisely at three thirty p.m., the time of their planned assignation, she saw the thin legs of Mrs. Elphinstone carefully descending the area steps. She nodded her approval as she crossed to the kettle to put the switch now onto 'boil'. People of quality were never late, she ruminated. Or as her dear mother used to insist: punctuality was the prerogative of princes...

She sighed. Normally this would have provoked opportunity for a nostalgic reverie over her mother who had died of sunstroke on August the Third, 1914, the day prior to the proclamation of the Great War. Thus she had never known the new motorized and airborne age, her daughter often mused.

But the door knocker was being used to announce Mrs. Elphinstone's arrival. There was no time now for a fond excursion down memory lane! With a quick touch to her henna'd head, to ensure the hairpins in the bun at the nape of her neck were in place, Daphne Hewlett-Whyte tottered to the door to receive her first purely social visitor since long before Hubert had departed his native land those five years earlier. Since that time Daphne always met people socially, *away* from the flat — on the mere handful of occasions that had presented themselves, that is...

Mrs. Elphinstone would not — although invited — use her volition over where to sit. So Daphne took the little cardtable chair and gave her guest the only upholstered one. Then she made the tea and pushed in the tea-trolley with its willow plate containing four fingers of sandwiches made with Shipham's bloater paste, and a pedestalled dish bearing the sponge cake she had made the previous Sunday, intending at the time to protract its consumption over the following week or so...

The conversation at first was most innocuous and rather more guarded than their initial one in the butcher's shop. Nevertheless Daphne did learn a few more salient facts about her visitor and vouchsafed her a comparable number of her own. Both women were widows, both torn in the previous century — although by a piece of rapid mental arithmetic allied to a reference to Queen Victoria's Diamond Jubilee, Daphne decided that her guest was at least six or seven years her senior; thuis closer to ninety than eighty. The toque, which she had not removed, suggested the nonagenerian fact, but the china blue eyes and soft cream skin did not.

Some people have all the luck, thought Daphne; then dismissed the notion as unworthy and unfair to this woman whom she would dearly like to encourage as a friend.

They had consumed the sandwiches and were toying with the sponge when the talk took an unexpected twist. Both women spoke of their children. "My son, Hubert, my only child, is at present in Canada, lecturing," Daphne volunteered.

"I, too, have but one child. His name is Meredith and he lives in retirement in Marakeesh — the last place of his employment with the Consular Service."

"What an extraordinary coincidence!" pursued Daphne. "Both only sons, and one of Hubert's travel books is on Morrocco. After tea, perhaps you would like to glance at one or two of his volumes. He is the author of several, you know. He was a great friend of Norman Douglas. As a matter of fact he met Norman through me, as he did so many brilliant authors of my generation. Willie Maugham thought the world of him."

Mrs. Elphinstone at this point lowered her teacup back into its saucer. "I take it from the names of his friends that you mention that your son is unmarried."

Mrs. Hewlett-Whyte nibbled unconcernedly at her sponge which she had layered sparingly with her favorite apricot jam. "Oh, you know these artistic ones! I really don't think Hubert has ever had the time to settle down and raise a family."

"Meredith had the time but not the inclination," her companion said firmly. "He has preferred co-habiting with other men. And, if I am not mistaken, that would seem to be the case with your Hubert."

This was not a constituent of conversation that Daphne found at all congenial. "Yes, well I *never* discuss my son's life — not even with him," she added meaningfully. "Now do tell me about your time in Paris. I knew la Belle France so well before the war. We had a lovely little place at Beaulieu on the Côte d'Azur. That was in the spring of 1924."

Mrs. Eleanor Elphinstone looked into the middle distance, her pale blue eyes looking paler than ever. "It was sheer misery. I hate the French for their rudeness, their arrogance, and their xenophobic ignorance. My son did not make things any easier with his tapettes at the dinner table and his excesive drinking afterwards. Always having to smile and be gracious to whatever urchin he dragged in from the local pissoir." She finally turned to look at Daphne. "I gather your son did not bring his friends home to meet mother? You are fortunate, my dear — at least in that respect. You have much reason for content."

If Daphne was squeamish about acknowledging Hubert's antics with other men, she was nevertheless highly competitive when it came to claims as to the degree of misfortune meted out to her in the course of life. "Just look about you," she replied, her voice rising. "I did not always live in such squalor. Hunert's private habits became even more expensive as he grew older."

"He had to pay more to satisfy his lust," said Mrs. Elphinstone flatly. "And you provided the financial source. Like many of these men he has been unable to contend successfully in the world."

Mrs. Hewlett-Whyte rose from her hard chair in consternation, flitted across to the mantelpiece, back to the curtained windows, and even described a rough pirouette. "Oh, I don't think you understand, Mrs. Elphinstone. I don't think you grasp what I'm saying one little bit! Hubert is a most *successful* author. There are three of his books in the Islington Public Library. Others, of course, are now out of print. And he never, never, embarassed me here with his private life."

"I was never embarassed by Meredith. Only angered. I was also humiliated when he would buy his boys expensive silk shirts and pigskinned and string-backed gloves from Medelios when I had too few francs to buy even the cheaper forms of *charcuterie* for the table. My clothes, including those you see me in now, came from the jumble sales of the various English-speaking churches in Paris. Fortunately, I had the consolations of religion, otherwise I might have gone under."

The conversation was progressively bothering Daphne. It was certainly not the kind of talk she had envisaged for two ladies sharing a common cultural and social background. "The Tuileries!" she exclaimed suddenly. "I have always adored their spaciousness."

But Eleanor Elphinstone was proving relentless. "One of Meredith's favorite sites for importuning," she said conversationally. "For that reason alone I hated them."

Mrs. Hewlett-Whyte tried even harder. "Le Jardin d'Acclimatation — at the bottom of the Avenue de la Grande Armée — what a sweet little zoo it housed!"

"Meredith took me there one May Day with a pouf named Jean-Luc who bought me the traditional sprig of muguet for that day. I can smell that Lily-of-the-Valley now... But the boy was neurotic and flirted with strangers to embarass and humiliate my son. I felt a pawn between them and was glad when their lust rekindled and they hurried me home to my siting room and my own devices whilst they sought a mattress."

That longish utterance wholly disconcerted Daphne who had now returned to her upright chair and was playing with the rings on her withered fingers. She had been precipitate, she told herself: allowing this woman over her threshold on too flimsy evidence of shared tastes and enthusiasms. "I don't want to hear of your pansy son," she cried. "Hubert is a gentleman. He is a successful writer, very highly esteemed in literary circles."

But Eleanor Elphinstone, having finally returned to and finished devouring her piece of sponge cake, and again holding her cup and saucer, proceeded as if her hostess were but a complaisant listener. "Of course, the father was weak. Then most of those who survived the war, were. The best being taken. A drunkard, and owning to grotesque vanity over his pretty-boy face. I am a strong woman, temperate and long-suffering. We women did not have our finest creamed off in slaughter like the men. So you can call Meredith a textbook case, I suppose, for an effeminate issue. I saw it all coming a long time ago. I could see the pederasty in that child before he owned a razor. Only back in those days it did not matter — Hamish would be the provider of grandchildren; preserve the name."

Her voice had dropped in key; grown softer, dreamier. But Daphne, following every hateful word, was aware of the novel name in the woman's monologue. "Hamish?" she queried sharply. "But you said your son's name was Meredith. This was another? You had *two* then!"

Eleanor sat up, stiff with opposition; the reverie banished. "A slip of the tongue. My son's name is Meredith. A retired Consular official living in North Africa with God knows what! My only boy whom I cherish in spite of his weaknesses."

"No! No!" Daphne protested. "There was no mistake. You had two sons. This one and one whom you admired more because he could have given you grandchildren. It is you who fear reality — not me!"

"Your son is a pouf, a sodomite, — who conceals it from a mother who is only too willing to remain ignorant. I at least acknowledge the truth of mine, even if I despise him and love him at one and the same time. Don't you see? We share the identicial affliction. We are two old women with pansy sons. We should belong to some kind of fiendish club."

Daphne Hewlett-Whyte now found strength where before it was all pain and reluctance. "Your normal son? What happened to him?

Something dreadful, was it? Something you refuse to think about any more?"

A pause mounted between them, so that both heard the clock ticking, as well as the sound of their own tired hearts. It was Eleanor Elphinstone who broke the silence.

"An aeroplane crash," she announced dully. "1936. A trip to Kitzbuhl for the skiing. Hamish was eighteen."

"Hubert once knew a boy named Hamish," Daphne said slowly. "He wore goggles and a leather jacket, and rode a motor-bike." She paused momentarily to take in breath. "He was *very* expensive. That is when we lost the companion chair to the one you are sitting in. And the nice dinner service that my mother-in-law had bequeathed to me from Arlington Hall, the family place. But before him there had been just the one person, for ever so long. His name was Roger and he and Hubert — oh, it must have been twelve, fifteen years they were together. But I never met him."

"Never," Mrs. Elphinstone repeated mechanically.

"I did not wish to," Daphne explained. "It — it was a side of Hubert I did not wish to explore."

"I would have liked to know much less than I learned from keeping a home for my son. But the bliss of such ignorance was denied me. I envy you."

"I envy you," said Daphne Hewlett-Whyte, "because you know where your son is and I do not. Only that he has reached a city called Vancouver and no longer writes. I think he will never forgive me over Roger and that the ones on whom he lavished gifts were really just to spite me. I do not expect to see my son again."

"This is a very painful conversation for us both," Mrs. Elphinstone announced. "But we must not depress each other. I would like another cup of tea if there is one under the cosy."

There was and Daphne poured it. Soon after that Mrs. Elphinstone enquired the whereabouts of the lavatory. When she emerged she made it obvious that she would not sit down again and was prepared to go.

"I liked you the minute I saw you in the butcher's," Daphne said, escorting her guest towards the door. "I have so enjoyed our little tea. You must really come again. We have so very much in common and that is not always the case, nowadays."

"Some conversations start auspiciously but this one did not," said the older of the two ladies. "I am sure, though, that we will meet again by virtue of our patronizing the same merchants."

However, internally, Eleanor Elphinstone was telling herself that Daphne Hewlett-Whyte was quite wrong. That gentility and pansy sons might well be shared, but that really all they had in common was the cruel weight of the years and unsatisfactory memories. She knew they would never share confidences again.

VANCOUVER SUMMER PUDDING

Take a bowl of fresh ripe blackberries adding sugar to taste. Around the interior of bowl lay slices of thinly cut white sandwich bread. Lay further slices across open top of bowl thus covering the fruit. Cover with greaseproof paper and a plate small enough to fit inside of bowl rim and on top of greaseproof. Then put either old-fashioned flat-iron or two or three bricks as weights on plate. Place bowl in refrigerator for thirty-six hours. Take bowl out, remove weights, and turn upside down on serving platter. The result should be a bowl-shaped pudding with exterior bread slices now molded into pudding shape and saturated with fruit juices from the blackberries. Serve in cut portions and add whipped cream.

We first noticed Richard and Anna when blackberry picking in Vancouver's Jericho Park on a hot day at the tail end of July. Ken and I were equipped simply with plastic bags from the nearby Safeway. They were prone to puncture on the bramble thorns so that we had to be extra careful in holding them high above the leaves when craning for the tall-growing fruit or away from the runners which disappeared into the long grass where we knew that there were yet more berries in plentiful supply.

But the Cobhams were altogether more professional. For one thing they carried walking sticks which they used with their handles inverted to lower some of the higher growing berries. And they put their blackberries into stiff straw baskets, the likes of which I hadn't seen since leaving England thirty years earlier. Even their apparel accorded better with berry collecting than did our garments. Then we were trying to combine this operation with walking two dogs, and Ken had come straight from the university campus and was wearing his teaching clothes. I was imprudently wearing an easily stained white shirt with short sleeves which left my arms readily vulnerable to savage scratching from the briars all about us.

The four of us were not alone. The edges of the park near the pond sites were adjacent to an old people's home and there were several of its inmates busily picking for the tarts and pies which would remind some of them of distant childhoods and prairie summers — for many, I had learned on our regular dogwalks, were retired Saskatchewan and Alberta farmers; immigrants, like me, to British Columbia. The bond was the past — and the special pleasure of harvesting things that mankind had not cultivated. There was a bent old man in a black beret with a white-haired wife with gnarled, clawing hands, joined in the mute intensity of their husbandry. And at one small, isolated patch, a frail, grand-motherly person frantically picking for a lazier generation (or so I imagined) who would visit on Sundays, eagerly wolf a piece of home-made pie but talk of jogging and gyms.

But it wasn't the oldsters who had ultimately engaged our attention;

nor the unruly kids who bent and broke a hundred tangled vines to pick a random berry and pop it between stained lips before passing, like a herd of giraffes, to the next unravaged clump. No, our interest was fired by this youngish couple who were working just a little apart from each other, but shouting every now and then to indicate fresh blackberries along the narrow path.

It was from her calling to him that I realised she was not a native English-speaker. But it was not, in fact, until a second encounter at a different site the following week that I learned she was German and that she was Anna, and he Richard and that their married name was Cobham. It was Ken who collected all that information — while I was busy rounding up an errant Springer spaniel puppy from the railway tracks under the Burrard bridge and holding on to a straining Norwegian Elkhound who rarely agreed with me over directions to take.

If it had been hot when picking at Jericho it seemed doubly so at this spot which was slightly further from any breeze from the sea. Here the brambles grew like breakers of greenery amid a sea of masonry and concrete which in turn threw the heat waves back at those who walked along the cinder path. I told a sweating Ken that I could scarcely remember when a cloud last crossed eastward across that remorseless sky. The vast sprawl of Vancouver wilted under the exigent heat as it grew progressively dusty and untidy. The hot days of sun brought crowds to the parched lawns of the city parks for which a niggardly council had refused sprinklers. The containers of waste were never sufficiently emptied to the point where the litter at their base was completely removed. Irresponsible dogowners allowed their animals to roam freely and deposit excrement where tanned youths and little children played. Drains smelled and the still air of the beaches was laced with unpleasant odors from the exposed giant sewers that reached out to sea. Not so privately, I declared our usually attractive city a mess and I can testify that every blackberry picked during those oppressive afternoons was washed, and washed, and washed again.

When a perspiring and irate me caught up with Ken after chasing Leila and lugging Leif up the steep railroad embankment I came across the three of them, picking and animatedly chatting. The bushes where they stood were particularly dusty and there was an unpleasant abundance of yellowing sheets of discarded newspapers impaled on various bushes and shrubs. It was not an attractive spot but the blackberries grew on both sides of the trail and were large and ripe and plentiful. Nobody else seemed to have discovered the place for a quick glance assured me there were none of those diminutive empty cups, paler than the surrounding greenery, as telltale evidence of berries picked from the same bushes.

I gave the Cobhams much closer scrutiny than the bushes as Ken introduced us and conversation picked up once more. The woman, Anna, now that I knew she was German, took on distinctly Nordic characteristics. She was blonde-haired, blue-eyed, and in her blue check blouse and denim skirt, looked cool and smart in spite of the heat and her exertion. I noticed when she picked berries above her that her armpits were unshaven — although her brown legs disappearing stockingless into loafers, were smooth enough. She was an ex-kindergarten teacher, I learned, and her husband a geneticist at the University of British Columbia. He had been born in Bristol and still had a vestigial British accent although his family, apparently, had moved to BC when he was a highschool student. I estimated they were both in their early thirties. They lived only six blocks from us in Kitsilano.

An adonis Richard Cobham was not. But what I did find appealing was his indubitable charm. The ready grin under the shock of unruly hair which fell across his forehead, shared pride of place with sparkling eyes. He also owned a snub nose and slim body. The latter, I sensed, spelled a questing energy which appeared consonant with his frequent spurts of laughter. Later I was to construe all that winsome youthfulness in quite another way, but not as we stood there, the four of us, playfully competing for the number of blackberries we were able to gather. Richard had the fullest basket — then he had the tallest reach and was the fastest at picking the fruit from its thorny branches. And all the time he talked, including me now in his audience.

"Anna is a lousy cook, in spite of her being European. I think that's why she went to Montreal where I met her. By *their* standards and their ghastly pig pie — that *tourtière* — she's haute cuisine, cordon bleu, anything you bloody well like! Have either of you ever had that horrible disappointment in Quebec? You look at a menu and there it all is, just as you'd find *à la carte* in Beaune or Bordeaux. Until the stuff arrives on the table and you find the French language has been camouflaging crappy old Canadian "greasey spoon". What a fucking disappointment when that first happens to you!" "Richard! Please mind your language. Not everyone appreciates your cussing."

We both reassured her that it didn't matter. It was obvious that it didn't matter to Richard either. Certainly she wasn't going to deter him or his vocabulary.

"Anyway, compared to *une tarte de bleuets Gaspésienne* her blackberry flan is better than a slab of shit. You guys must come over and try it. She won't mind trying her feeble culinary skills before a couple of men, will you my love?" Anna grinned ruefully. "You don't cook?" she asked me. "Only water," I told her. "Ken does it all. Mind you," I added quickly, "we both make a point of not choosing friends for their cooking talents. Nor for their athletic prowess, arable skills, fecundity or nautical abilities, come to that."

They both laughed and I was relieved. I didn't like seeing a man putting down his wife — or vice versa. But I also noticed that my words inspired Mr. Richard Cobham to give us an extra sizing up. I wondered just how much Ken had told them about us before I had arrived with the dogs. I was pretty sure it was very little, knowing Ken....

"And cards, too, I hope," Richard supplemented, as his questing look embraced my roommate as well as myself. "Anna and I are hopeless at all card games — and that includes scrabble, monopoly and bloody bridge."

"We shoot people and bury them under the kitchen floor if they arrive at our house even *carrying* a deck of cards," I told him.

Richard may not have liked cards but it was very evident that he loved playing games — English parlor games.

"OK" he shouted (then he rarely spoke more quietly out there in the open air) "Let's see what else we can agree on. How about Anna's stepmother — the biggest bitch in Christendom. You must've read about her. She's in the Guinness Book for bitchery!"

"Darling, don't be extravagant," Anna pleaded. "You'll have both Ken and Davey thinking you're madder than you really are."

"I really am amazed that no one has found this lot of blackberries before us," Ken said pacifically.

"People are blind," Richard said roughly. "And bloody stupid to boot. They don't only miss blackberries, though. They let the goddamn Americans go on preparing to blow up the world." He sounded so savage, in fact, that I stopped picking — and as I did so, let a particularly thorny bramble swing back and slash my bare arm which was upraised to protect my face. Although we stood in the shade the air was still warm and motionless: nevertheless I felt the extra warmth immediately upon my exposed skin. I looked down. A rash of red beads burgeoned as the scratch flowered into bloody blossom.

Richard was at once all anxiety. "Jesus! That looks nasty! Here, use this." He pulled a Kleenex pack from the army satchel at his feet. But his wife was at his side in an instant. She, too, rummaged in the bag and brought out a small bottle of Dettol, surgical cotton and a package of Elastoplasts.

She pushed her husband aside. "Here, let me have a look."

"It doesn't hurt," I told her as she wiped away the first installment of blood and then applied the disinfectant.

"And I'm sure it's clean," I added.

"You can't be too careful," she warned. "Anyway, I took first-aid once and I love to practice. Ask Richard. The smallest cut and I've got him swathed in bandages."

"Thank God I'm a hypochondriac," he said with another grin.

"It has kept our marriage together for six years. She's a frustrated doctor, you see — and I'm a potentially perpetual patient. It works beautifully."

She put the largest Elastoplast over the surgical wool so that my scratch was entirely covered. "That's how *he* puts it," she said, looking up into my face. She was close enough for me to receive the faint smell of her sweat. "It's really a mother-son relationship, I always tell him he passed from his mother to me without even noticing the difference."

I was to recall her remark subsequently.

"There you are," she concluded. "I think you'll live now."

"No septicemia?"

"No septicemia," she confirmed.

"The dogs are bored with blackberry picking," Ken announced, from which I inferred that he was, too.

"Well, we have enough for that summer pudding," I told him. "Summer pudding?" Richard echoed. "What in hell is that?" Ken threw me a familiar look. He had guessed what I was about to say — and didn't welcome it. He knew I was about to offer an invitation. And he has never encouraged me in dragging home everyone I ever meet — which I am rather prone to do, I admit. But the summer heat acted upon my ever-ready perversity in spite of his mute discouragement.

"How about coming to our place tomorrow and finding out? It won't be a heavy supper in this weather but Ken promised me a Vancouver summer pudding if I went blackberrying again. We call it "Vancouver" simply because we use Vancouver blackberries.

It wasn't Ken's way to resolve our differences in public. Instead he looked carefully and at length at our two transparent bags. "Davey's right," he said eventually. "There's enough for a pudding and for freezing in a pie as well. How about a light supper, then? Eight o'clock? We can eat outside in this weather. And then Davey can entertain you as I shall have probably to go indoors and finish an article I keep putting off."

Anna answered for both of them. Very quickly. "You look as if you are very punctual," she said to him. "Eight on the dot, right?"

Ken nodded. His face was expressionless and I felt a mild irritation in his refusal to look a little more encouraging. Then that and the threat of leaving me to play host was the price he was making me pay for his concurrence. His reproofs are never very exorbitant...

In any event it was closer to eight-thirty the next evening when they arrived. So much for her "on the dot" routine, and my notions of Germanic punctuality. We had laid the bright check tablecloth under the wisteria-festooned arbor, lit four candles, brought out the wine in its terra-cotta cooler, and switched on the garden lights just as the summer dusk was gathering.

Ken surveyed our handiwork as we awaited the click of the gate latch or the barking of the dogs — whichever came first. "Though I say it myself, it does all look quite attractive," he commented.

I remembered our Connecticut days. "In the east," I added, "we would have also lit the citronella candle, squirted *Raid* everywhere and rubbed *Off* on our bare arms and necks. Thank God for westcoast freedom from mosquitoes!"

Our shared complacency spilled like an invisible essence over the white metal garden chairs drawn up at the table on which Ken had placed a vase of sweet scented stock whose perfume filled the warm air.

From the road beyond the front of our house we heard a car pull up and its engine switch off. The dogs heard, too, and the canine din savaged the suburban quiet. Ken fled indoors to stir a pot while I hastened to the side gate lest our visitors be unduly scared by the racket from the dogs. I should perhaps have immediately suspected something by the noticeable change in demeanour in both of them since our shared blackberry picking. His boyish ebullience was withheld and no staccato torrent of words accompanied that faintly British accent when he greeted me. Indeed, he seemed petulant and it was Anna who had now become the chatterbox. Even before we were seated she had lavished praise on the garden setting, admired the now-quietened dogs, and twice informed us how fortunate they felt in being invited.

Ken and I exchanged looks. He kept on demurring at her unstinted encomiums by shaking his head and making lots of polite noises in his throat. After some fifteen minutes of all this her husband seemed to change his mind and came to life — vigorously.

"Dogs," he announced. "When they aren't shitting everywhere they've got their noses up each others asses before coming and licking you. They're filthy!"

Ken and I remained silent. Leif and Leila stayed at our feet: impervious. Anna, though, smiled sweetly at this sudden outburst. "Then you agree with me after all, Darling. They're no substitute for children. I think you are absolutely right! The maternal instinct shouldn't be sublimated by animals."

"That's not what I bloody well said, dammit! If dogs are plain anti-social, then having kids is grotesquely irresponsible with the Bomb around the corner."

Ken stood up. "I'll get some more white wine from the fridge." "If everyone talked like my husband," Anna remarked, looking at me as the only possible ally left, "there'd be no mankind to save from the nuclear war in a few years. I want a baby, you see, Davey. We can work out the nuclear problems afterwards." For one ludicrous moment I thought she might be actually making me a proposal but I was saved from idiotic comment by Richard erupting again.

"You wouldn't, you silly bitch, if you could imagine a fried infant or some lunatic monstrosity with cancerous lesions thrown in. Let's get *total* nuclear disarmament — and then we can talk about upping the birthrate. Do you know those bloody dogs can breed twice a year? If the Yanks get their way and use the bomb the world is soon going to be over-run with radioactive, mad dogs!"

A silence ensued. I made no effort to dispell it — guessing correctly that ultimately Anna would.

Out of the blue she asked what I thought of a recent play by Janice Ripley, an earnest local playwright. I started to say that I had mildly enjoyed it when Richard interrupted to say he thought it stupid, old fashioned, and uncommitted to the basic issues of the times we were living through.

His opinions were one thing — bullying me with them quite another. "I gather you're not enthusiastic," I interjected with as much sarcasm as I could muster. (Which is actually quite a lot.) "It is certainly the most *direct* of her plays I've seen. No one could call it abstruse."

"No one in our circles would call *anything* abstruse," said Richard, with what I read as a nasty smile.

"My male chauvinist husband wouldn't like it anyway, because it's by a woman," Anna put in. "But I have to say I didn't care for it much either. It was too sentimental. But perhaps being European the play is just too North American for me."

"I think she's English-born and Jewish," I said, trying to simmer less with her.

"It's amazing, isn't it, how the Yanks can be so sloppily sentimental and yet so cynical with their aggressive imperialism and threats to destroy our planet." Richard stuck his thumb in the lapel of his jacket and leaned back on his chair across from me. I wondered if he was still irritated with me for using the word "abstruse".

I was saved further speculation by Ken's return. He had obviously heard much of our conversation crossing the lawn. "I think you're all making mountains out of vicious little molehills. Isn't the play about broken dreams and womanly dilemmas? I would've thought that still relevant in 1984 and the dilemmas have male equivalents, too."

Richard was eyeing his wife now. His look was not amiable. "Of course you could have told the thing was by a woman, even without a program. Only a woman could drip all that martyrdom. Or the penis-envy, come to that!"

"Anyone mind if I put on a Beethoven quartet?" I asked, suiting action to words and crossing to the outdoor stereo and searching for a cassette from the pile we had brought out before the advent of our guests.

"What, no Kenneth McKellar?" Richard asked, once more rocking back on his chair.

The business of putting on the E-Flat piano quartet saved me the onus of response. By the time I returned to the table the bickering between Richard and Anna had quickened and was to remain a constant throughout the rest of the evening. I must confess, however, that it impinged less and less upon me as they battled babies and bombs through Ken's home-made pâté, a shrimp omelette, and subsequent spinach salad — right up to the Summer Pudding: the ostensible reason for our assembly. As I listened to Richard's anti-American diatribe with increasing distaste I eyed his tautly handsome face and wondered if similar thoughts and attitudes had once coursed angrily through my brain — when my hair had been as devoid of grey as his and my skin as tightly smooth.

Such reflections were becoming depressingly familiar. More and more frequently I found myself slipping outside the confines of argument, escaping even a moral stance over things, to reflect instead on the *motivations* of those who championed this cause or that and to consider (albeit sadly) whether or not I had given up personal convictions to be, instead, a mere recorder and reflector of the passion and commitment of others. I had, on occasion, brought these musings to Ken's notice, but he had invariably dismissed them as foolish if not self-pitying.

This was a night when I was again tempted to repeat my misgivings to him. When they finally left, after two large post-dinner scotches (which I felt Richard could have well done without) we two sat there in the semi-darkness and made desultory conversation of a post-mortem nature over our departed guests.

"At least he really believes in his causes — however crudely he shouts them," I said. "I couldn't get that het up over anything."

But Ken was neither minded to defend Richard, nor let me off the hook. He tapped his fingers uncharacteristically on the tabletop. "That's nonsense, Kiddo. You can be as argumentative as the next when you want to be. Most of your friends would laugh their heads off if they heard you say that. As for him — nothing excuses the way he talks to her. Nothing! I don't *care* how committed he is to his bloody causes, that's no way to treat a friend, let alone a wife."

I stared towards Ken, even though I could scarcely make out his features since we had doused the guttering candles. "He really did get to you, didn't he? I thought I was the only one thinking what an idiot he was making of himself — even if I did admire the fire he could stoke up."

There was a silence and I sensed that agin I had brushed Ken the wrong way. I wasn't mistaken.

"That's half your trouble, Davey. Of course you thought you were the only one. Then at times like tonight you tend to act as if you *were* the only one out here."

I bridled at once. "Well, you hardly helped matters. You never once came to her rescue when he attacked her. If you ask me, you were sulking because they didn't make more fuss over your Vancouver summer pudding."

"I'm not talking about what I did or didn't do. That isn't the subject at the moment. Nor does the summer pudding come into it. I could see right away that neither of them much cared about what they ate. It's an instinct we cooks soon develop and which I suspect you know nothing about."

Being barely capable of boiling an egg, I was not going to contend with him in that quarter. "If you'd only speak up and say what you think while people are still around it wouldn't put me in such an egotistical light. As it is, I always appear the argumentative one and you the cool, objective type who disdains the cut and thrust of debate."

"We're not debating now, Davey. We're bickering! And that puts us on a par with the likes of the Cobhams."

I saw an escape from an incipient quarrel. "Well, Bonzo," (using my personal nickname for him) "I don't think I'm about to call you a bitch, tell you not to have children, and to drown the dogs."

When Ken laughed, even if it was short and strained, my spirits rose. Crisis averted. We rounded the evening out in the garden with a final scotch apiece and then took the dinnerware indoors, stacked the yard furniture and finally sauntered inside to bed.

As if an unspoken truce had been established, neither of us made more than scanty reference to either of them in the days that followed. Nor did we grumble when they failed to phone or in any way mark their appreciation of the Summer Pudding evening.

I think that both Ken and I felt that in some mysterious way the fractious couple had made negative impact upon us. It was only too easy, for instance, for me to see myself a little like a craven version of Richard, and I had the sense that Ken could as easily see himself sufficiently akin to Anna to be uncomfortable with the comparison. Fanciful perhaps. But that was it. Those oddball two made me feel strangely guilty and I could believe that Ken didn't like the idea of me thinking he was a bit like Anna in ducking from issues by embracing the prosaic.

But the whole matter was rendered rather academic when, some two weeks later, we were again walking the dogs and again in search for blackberries as ingredients for more Vancouver summer puddings. This time, though, the venue was in the southern heights of Jericho park; in the vicinity of Fourth Avenue where through bramble bushes, sappling willows and tall clumps of broom, could occasionally be seen glimpses of the Justice Institute above the slopes on the far side of the divided thoroughfare.

Not that either of us looked at or even spared a thought for that road and Jericho hill which bordered it to the south. Where we stood picking was a world very much its own. Quite free of other pickers we seemed alone with the cheerful sounds of redwing blackbirds and the occasional chatter of a pair of pheasants we knew inhabited the dense scrubland surrounding us. The dogs also seemed to respond to this isolated tract above the marshes by staying close at hand and not persistently reminding us they preferred running to standing by bramble bushes which had such arcane attractions for their two masters.

At an earlier time in the year the nearby slopes were carpeted with blue lupin interspersed with white daisies. But in this August cocoon of heat there was only limp green as minor perforation to the tawny hillsides of hay, and the very first intimations of an approaching fall in the glow of crimson amid the yellowed leaves of the sumac. The air was still, the blackberries magnificently large in their unpicked plenty. We were contentedly self-absorbed as our Safeway plastic bags grew ever more swollen with their purple and our fingers ever more mauve in the stain of their juice.

Then, very faintly, as if from somewhere far, far from where we labored, we heard singing. We exchanged glances mystified — perhaps even resentful of the vocal trespassing. The dogs appeared to ignore the sound of distant massed voices, although it grew stronger every second. Instead they looked from one of us to the other, wagged their tails, and probably hoped we would at least move on from that one gigantic bush where we had lingered for nearly twenty minutes.

But we didn't. We just picked our berries more slowly. As the sound grew louder we could make out the tune and recognize some of the words. Our curiosity was piqued as we realized we were listening to the refrain from "We Shall Overcome".

"A labor demonstration?" I suggested.

"A Peace March, more likely," Ken offered — and, as it proved, more accurately. It seemed a long time before the procession was anywhere near us. Before that, we had already decided to edge a little closer to view the marchers. By now I had indeed abandoned berrying and with my bulging bag at my side, stood there awaiting them, my head stuffed with thoughts. This is no place to embark on a political essay but I can't help stating that my mind and emotions were once more in acute conflict. Then as now, I ached for the same goals as those strenuously singing "We Shall Overcome". I wanted The Bomb buried, the missiles abandoned, all nuclear weapons proscribed across the globe. I wanted, I prayed, for the peace of the world. Yet even as my heart stirred and I felt exhilarating solidarity with vulnerable mankind who simply wished to escape the thrall of the bellicose generals, I knew a bitter sense of Giant Manipulation at work. Oh yes, I could see so vividly the radio-active desert, the skinless dead, the living remnants of children. I would yield to none in the nightmare vision of man's inhumanity to man. After all, was it not my own generation who had revealed the moral stain of centuries in unveiling the stinking suppuration of the death camps and, within a matter of months, burned the lids from the eyes of myriads in Hiroshima and Nagasaki?

But try as I might, I could not shove my head in the morass of a nightmare Armageddon and leave my commonsense aside in the cause of salvation from a man-wrought Apocalypse. I could shudder at the prospect of an insupportable future but in the same breath I had to swell with ire at the perception of a cynical Marxist orchestration of fear and anger in the totalitarian cause of false-peace.

Of course there was the unthinkable horror of nuclear oblivion — but there was also the thinkable nadir of freedomless reality in those arid countries I had visited where friends sadly wrote off today in the faint promise of tomorrow. And I knew that the two were linked and I knew that *"better red than dead"* was the saddest twentieth century reflexion and the bottom line of moral bankruptcy. I was saved more bitterly paradoxical thought by Ken's bending down, clipping on Leif's leash, and calling out to me to move closer to him so that I, too, could see what my ears now told me was a vast concourse of people.

There they were, massed untidily across the four lanes of roadway, but protected by a police escort which both preceded and flanked them. I started to count but soon gave up. There were thousands — surely over fifty thousand, perhaps even one hundred thousand marching below the Justice Institute having earlier passed the Canadian Army barracks and with Jericho Hill School for the Deaf on the ridge peering down at them....

Later the media seemed unanimous in stating that it was the largest demonstration of its kind in Vancouver's century of existence. It was stated proudly, too. My sense was that everyone was proud of the fact that our westcoast city evoked an infinitely more numerous response to anxiety over nuclear destruction than either Toronto or Montreal which were both roughly double the size.

But I run ahead of myself. Suddenly I hear a dog chain chink as Ken grabs my arm. "Look," he shouts, "Look at the line just come into sight. The fourth and fifth persons nearest our side. See?"

I did. Immediately. In fact without his help I had already blotted out a multitude as two loomed for me as for him. There walk Anna and Richard. They are holding hands, swinging them in unison — which is how we can see they are joined. But it is their faces which nail our attention. Their expression — for the look is identical — is blissful. They are singing together, their lips thus also in unison. Both heads are held very high, their marching bodies taut with pride and youth. Just as they draw abreast of where we stand, invisible to them, they look at each other and I look straight into the eyes of Richard, dog-hater and lover of humanity. I have never read such happiness in a human face. They stop singing. They have to — for the look into each other is quickly followed by a kiss. Brief, because of the momentum of marching, but meaningful for all that....

A further refrain was launched from the head of the column: Refuse the Cruise! It was straightway picked up by the waves of peace-walkers. I saw the lips of our Summer Pudding guests take up the defiant shout, but the joy never left their eyes. Then, with an abruptness that I found oddly shocking, it was all over. We found ourselves looking only at the napes of necks, unknown faces, or male and female flowing hair.

9

THE VANCOUVER SPECTRE

In a part of town we Vancouverites don't boast about a recumbent figure lay in an empty lot and let his urine seep through his pants and stain the front page of a month-old Vancouver *Sun* which seemed to ill-serve him as a blanket. I know these particulars because I stumbled on the man as I dodged around a pile of litter as I hurried towards Chinatown and Dim Sung with a friend, David Wong, who was going to provide me with background material on silkscreen painting, in my role as art critic.

My foot had missed the unshaven face by inches. I looked down, full of apology; prepared, for once, to depart from a resolution never to give a wino money. I need not have worried at that moment about parting with loose change. The man's eyes were closed and the prone body in its ill-fitting Sally Ann suit, hadn't moved a hairsbreadth at the crunch of my shoes on the hard ground.

I noticed the short hair — just light enough to be called blond — was encrusted with blood. There was a whitish substance about his chest and knees which I realized with a start must be frost. He had presumably been lying there all night with the newspaper providing little protection. The article I was to write on Chinese art suggests that the year was 1968 or 1969. I also remember that it was March for I had been admiring some azaleas before disembarking from the bus and walking in that part of the city where no flowers grow.

I began to take in other details. Across the rumpled trouser of the lower part of his left leg was a narrow but shiny trail. Either a slug or snail had passed that way — presumably in frustrated quest for some vegetation which was absent from that patch of wasteland below the viaduct. But perhaps the most significant particular was one which eluded me at first. In fact my sight had wandered up and down his dishevelled body two or three times before I noticed it. His left ear, the only one which protruded because of the way he was lying, had a slice cut out of its lobe. It was no ordinary nick at that: not an accident from a hasty razor or even a botched job for an earring if the man was a mariner. (Remember, it was long before young men, punk or otherwise, routinely perforated one ear for the insertion of a small gold ring.) This was a distinct 'V' running from the lobe's circumference to the moulding shape of the stiffer cartilage. To my interested eye — perhaps more responsive that most to the odd or significant — it seemed no heirloom of a skid-road fracas or barroom brawl. It looked more like an act of nature; an inheritance congenitally conceived. That conclusion stemmed mainly from the nature of the blemish but I think also that my banishment of any suggestion of injury derived from altercation was strengthened by the faint but persistent aura of gentility emanating from the prostrate figure. So his clothes were indescribably filthy, he wore traces of blood and his stench, frankly was nauseating. But his hands were refined in their tapering fingers, his nails reasonably clean compared to the rest of him. And I have already referred to the fact his hair was neatly cut.

These speculations were abruptly severed when he suddenly opened his eyes and looked at me. I have rarely been the recipient of such contempt. "Had your fill?" he painfully croaked. "Then fuck off!"

"I'm sorry," I blurted — quite undone by that look of dismissiveness. Or was it hatred? "I didn't mean to tread on your hand. I'm afraid I wasn't looking where I was going when I came around that pile of trash."

He was not to be mollified. His sizing me up with one, raking glance had little in common with my careful estimation of him. I presume he noted my Harris tweed jacket, the Oxford shirt and crimson foulard scarf. "Fuck off poofta! Now go before I give you wings with a kick up the ass."

His language was crude, to say the least, and his term for me particularly unsettling because of the truth in it. But none of that prevented me from realizing that this wasn't some unlettered lout addressing me. At any rate, his response was instant and violent. "Now bugger off out of here," he roared, raising himself with difficulty to a half-recumbent position. "I don't want pooftas around me and I'm not a case for bloody social workers if you're one of them, too."

His voice was so loud I hastily looked about me to see if we were attracting attention. I began to panic. With difficulty, for I was now trembling, I got out my wallet and searched for money to silence his yelling. All I could find was a two dollar bill which I at once let flutter down. His gratitude was not to be bought. "About the bloody least you can do after walking over someone," he muttered, stuffing the orange-brown note somewhere in the folds of his suit. He was still grumbling to himself as I hastened away to the assignation with my friend who I knew would ridicule my attempts to buy off a foul-mouthed old bum whom I'd accidentally trodden on.

Actually, David Wong — apart from briefly scolding me for showering money on drunks — settled straight to the history of Chinese silkscreen painting. Then bums around Chinatown are old hat. Apart from telling my roommate, Ken, when he returned home from teaching at U.B.C. that day, the incident soon passed from my mind.

It was not to be resurrected until 1970 when Ken and I were attending an opening at The New Design Gallery. It was a *vernissage* for the painter Gresham Jones at the gallery's then location on Hornby Street which was to be usurped some years later by an Italian restaurant.

Jones had covered the walls of the converted frame house with the vibrant acrylic of his geometric debut in the hard-edged genre. The works fascinated me in that in spite of their depersonalised elegance and transcontinental derivation — like so many, he had come to the hard-edged image via magazines — I still felt I could perceive both something of the artist's personal signature and even an echo of regional locale in the large and lurid canvases.

Gresham Jones had always been popular, both with the public and his fellow painters, and I was not surprised to see the likes of such luminaries as Shadbolt, Smith, and Korner in the crowded surroundings. The exhibition had only been open an hour or so. (I had seen the show earlier that afternoon for the purposes of my reviewing) yet already canvas after canvas sported bright red stars of acquisition. That compounded my good spirits. Gresham was a decent man and a committed artist — even if he, like too many of his peers, succumbed excessively to other men's theories in those febrile times. I was glad to see him making a few thousand dollars after some twenty years of poorly paid recognition.

With my review under my belt and about to appear in *The Sun*, I had no hesitation in chatting with the other art patrons and of thus renewing both old and new relationships. On the top floor of the gallery we found a few of his recent watercolors in the same idiom and after a hasty consultation over whether we could afford a couple of hundred dollars our own red sticker was affixed to a cool oblong work in marine colors, which still adorns Ken's study. After some minutes of admiring our purchase I looked once more across the small room which I guessed had originally been maids' quarters when a simple attic. Through a scrummage of people — up there where the cheaper watercolors were housed it was particularly crowded — I saw my derelict again. He was no longer dressed as a skid-road bum, though, but more congruously with the New Design crowd, in a sports jacket with leather elbow-patches, plum-colored cords, and wore much longer hair than when sprawled on the deserted lot on the fringes of Chinatown.

What was wholly unchanged, however, was the glance of implacable hatred he at once accorded me. He was still thoroughly dishevelled in appearance and I again had the sense the man had been drinking heavily. He might be standing but I was again looking at an alcoholic wreck. I wanted to grab Ken's arm and point the stranger out but unfortunately my companion was blocked from me by another knot of people who had just climbed the steep stairs.

Then and there I decided to accost the man and bluntly ask if there was any good reason why he was eyeing me with such blatant vitriol. As I shoved forwards through the crowd he began to move away. His eyes still held me in their sight and I suddenly felt a shock as I discerned the now clean-shaven mouth abruptly frame the epithet 'poofta'.

It was at the very same moment that my sight fastened on that oddly nicked left earlobe. Tha provided an even greater impetus to confront him and I elbowed the fiercer at those in my way. In vain. When I arrived at the top of the stairs he had vanished. And a reckless bounding down two more flights — to a flurry of angry or startled glances — equally failed to raise him in my sights. The embarassing minutes spent after I returned from the rain-moist street and slowly climbed the three flights to re-join Ken were spent mumbling inanities and warding off solicitous enquiries as to whether the *Sun* art critic had been in pursuit of a pickpocket or merely lost his senses. But a fatuous grin for the public obscured an internal churning, where fear stirred.

* * *

All that was pretty much forgotten as the days and weeks elapsed and did not materialize afresh until over eighteen months had passed — and then in a far more tenuous fashion. My father had died and I had duly attended the funeral; our friend Elspeth had had a baby in the Kootenay Commune where she had gone to live with draft-dodger Chris, and we had a new Standard Poodle. Life moved on...

Raindrops chased each other down the plate-glass doors of the Queen Elizabeth Theatre as we milled about the foyer during an opera intermission. Sutherland was singing *Lucrezia Borgia* — and the evening was a chill one with the heavy downpour determining the desolation of the empty forecourt which was only marginally relieved by the reflected lights in the surface of the rain-lashed puddles.

The audience was as mixed as most of those for the Vancouver Opera Association, with the socialite groups of tuxedos and sequined gowns, standing as self-conscious islands between awed citizens in lounge suits, the impervious leather-and-onkh brigade of the period, and a substantial contingent of slim young men, penguined or otherwise, who laughed and nudged among themselves and perhaps held their plastic glasses more daintily than did the older and plumper establishment which sweated profusely from dinners too large or too rapidly consumed. The conversation, as I edged my way up and down the crowded foyer shamelessly eavesdropping, ranged from the knowledgeable to the idiotic.

I guess lots of us tend to be a little too self-aware on such occasions. I know I do. So it was with a broader smile, an extra spurt of enthusiasm, that I greeted such as the local impressario, Wayland Meredith, inclined my grinning head towards the most expensive interior decorator in town whose name I could never remember — and stopped gratefully to talk with Julius and Julia Hoffman, cultured Jews who had arrived on the scene thanks to Hitler and The *Anschluss*, and who were not only vital contributors to our flourishing opera company but had also been instrumental in the building of the civic theatre which housed it.

As part of the higher echelons in the lumber industry Julius could claim full membership of the Vancouver business community but with his wife's active role as a piano accompanist the couple were equally at home with those in the performing arts. They were unpretentious, energetically solicitous whenever Ken and I were ill, and as frequent attenders at our dinner table as we were at theirs. In short they were good friends and as I joined them and their semi-circle I felt somewhat less phony than when progressing down the entrance salon in their direction.

"Enjoying Big Joan?" Julius asked, "she sure is on form tonight, isn't she?"

"Frankly, I'm enjoying everything except the weather outside," I told him. "I hope the critics do, too. I don't want to read any more crap about how weak or creaky the plot is. But that's what always happens when my paper or the other sends sportswriters or church organists to cover things."

There was encouraging agreement from all around me. The Hoffmans and I had discussed this often before but it was good to see their friends, Lynn Copthorne, a recent widow, and her gay companion, Carlos Gonzales, an architect, were likewise nodding their heads. There was another man and woman I didn't know. Julia Hoffman seemed to anticipate my thought processes. "By the way, I'm not sure you've met Tina Choy who's visiting from San Francisco."

"No I haven't," I said, reaching out and shaking hands with the svelte Chinese woman. "Welcome to Vancouver and our weather! I'm afraid the opera sets would hardly satisfy Kurt Herbert Adler."

"On the other hand, I think Miss Sutherland is in better voice here than when I heard her last in the San Francisco Opera House," she said, smiling sweetly.

My eye finally reached the last person in the group, and again, Julia furnished the introduction. "And this is Harvey Stone — a friend of Tina's. He was just telling us before you arived how he remembers hearing the likes of Flagstad and Eva Turner at Covent Garden."

I wasn't listening. I was looking. The man she referred to was as huge and rumpled as his Chinese companion was slim and chic. I was quick to notice also that he was far from sober. Alcohol-reddened eyes gleamed from a pudgy face. There was something else about him, too, which I found disturbing. His greying hair was long and scurf made an unpleasant mantle to his dinner jacket. There was also an air of hostility stemming from him which seemed to be aimed largely in my direction. His words confirmed the impression.

"I certainly remember hearing better stuff that this provincial nonsense."

The antagonism I ignored. The voice I could not. It had a reedy hoarseness to it that I had previously heard. Yet the more I stared at him the more I realized I'd never set eyes on him before. The others had all fallen silent as he grated on with his attack on Canadian arts in general and this Vancouver production in particular. I think we were all relieved when the intermission bell sounded and it was time for the assembly to disintegrate.

I had just bidden goodbye to an embarassed all six of them (while Harvey Stone continued to emit his admonishments) when he took a podgy and surprisingly bejewelled hand to a lock of that unhealthy hair and removed it from his sweating forehead. I immediately saw that the gesture revealed an earlobe marked by a distinct 'V' nicked in its circumference. I stared powerlessly at him as he began to move towards the auditorium. I shook my head with disbelief. This Harvey Stone couldn't possibly have been the derelict from the lot. Stone's hair was as grey as the bum and the art patron's had been fair. Only those bloodshot eyes held the same animosity. And the voice, of course, I would have sworn on a stack of bibles it was identical. I did not have to hear this tuxedo'd operagoer say 'poofta' to know *precisely* how he would have sounded...

I stayed with Ken for the remaining intermission and told him excitedly of all that had happened and of the eerie re-incarnation of the mysterious figure now in a fresh guise after the skid row and the New Design Gallery mainfestations. I emphasized how he had railed at me and stared so vindictively. Frankly, Ken was not so disturbed as I was but it was to shortly transpire that this third incident had obviously made some impression on him. The very next day, when I got home from walking the dogs, I found him on the phone to Julia Hoffman. When, after what seemed at least an hour but could not have been more than twenty minutes, he finally replaced the receiver, he had a fund of interesting things to say about Harvey Stone with the intriguingly nicked earlobe.

"Leaving aside the business of coincidence, your Mr. Stone does have a rather interesting background."

"He's not *my* anything, " I remonstrated mildly.

Ken sat back in his armchair and eyed the glass of gin and tonic he'd poured himself while I was out. "I wouldn't be too sure of that. Not once you've heard about his sordid past and the scandal he once created in these parts."

"The suspense is killing me! Was he a murderer or something?"

"Not quite. But if he dared call you a poofta like your skid row friend he should've been donated the Hypocrite of the Year Award! Years ago, you see, he lived with another man. They were both youngish, I gather. Around thirty, say? Anyway, our Harvey gets ambitious and sees that his relationship is not proving much of a social asset in the Vancouver of the period."

"Which was?"

"Julia didn't exactly say. I gather sometime after WW2 — early fifties sounds right. So he takes up with a young socialite who if not pretty is as rich as Croesus. Her father was a lumber baron who himself had married into even more money. A local spice importer with a title — Belgian — in the background. Mama's family (the one with a Baron and Baroness in it and a fortune from the Belgian Congo) is snobbish and stuffy. They wanted their granddaughter, Mary, to marry something European. At least a Count. But I think an English remittance man would have done at a pinch. But quiet Mary proves stubborn. It's Harvey she wants and Harvey alone she's prepared to marry. Julia seemed vague as to the degree of opposition the family put up, but she says there were plenty of tales of tears and tantrums still going the rounds when she herself first came out from Edmonton where her family had settled after fleeing Austria.

"At any rate, Mary won out and the wedding duly went off. A really swell affair at Christ Church Cathedral with the Lieutenant Governor putting in an appearance and people like the Rodgers, the Buckerfields, and H.R. Macmillans. There's not much more social weight around here than that, as you know."

I nodded, thinking of half a dozen buildings bearing such names — although simultaneously realizing it was often hard to put a face to those kind of people. They donated money and monuments to the city but the wealthy we encountered on our hectic round of cultural events — the *vernissages*, concerts, theatre first-nights, and the like — were more inclined to comprise a less august philanthropic contingent.

"Then after the marriage the scandal really begins to pick up. Harvey Stone or his boyfriend (the point has never been clarified) decided that they couldn't stand to be alone, even for the length of a honeymoon. *So all three departed together.* The trio headed first for San Francisco, took a Matson Line ship to Hawaii, and finally showed up at The Empress in Victoria. By this time social Vancouver was in uproar. Snapshots were produced showing *à trois* picnics on tropical beaches and there was no lack of volunteers to swear they had observed the two men arm in arm in San Francisco. But by the return to British Columbia, family forces had recouped and renewed the attack. There are some irritating lacunae which I suspect will never be filled unless Harvey himself spills the beans, but Julia swears that only Mr. and Mrs. Harvey Stone disembarked from the Nanaimo ferry, and the implications are that the boyfriend was bought off.

That's not quite the end of the story, though. Mary and Harvey stayed together for less than a year and although they were never divorced they never put in a joint social appearance from that time on. Mary died five years ago and since then Harvey has developed a kind of elderly bachelor role and is seen at such things as the opera only in the company of women unlikely to be linked romantically with him. He has never, to Julia's knowledge, been seen publicly with another man from the time of his odd honeymoon."

I twirled my ice cubes in the drink I'd just made while listening to Ken. "At least it would explain his coldness towards the likes of me," I mused. "And I suppose it also accounts for his looking a typical local lush. My God, they drink hard in this town!" The thought made me decide not to have a second gin and tonic before dinner.

Which brings me almost to the present. I was on the campus of the University of British Columbia last week waiting for Ken to conclude his final afternoon lecture. I sat in the small alumni gardens adjoining Brock Hall. They are rather unkempt but it was a superb spring day and although the camelias were waning the later azaleas were at their most resplendent. It was warm enough in the April air to sit on the concrete bench (class of '28) and close my eyelids under the gentle sun. I don't know what persuaded me to suddenly open them again but by now you can perhaps guess who greeted me.

There on the opposite side of the flowers beds and lawns sprawled a large man with his legs apart and his arms outstretched along the back of his bench. H didn't look totally like the skid row apparition, nor would I have sworn he was exactly the same figure I'd encountered in The New Design Gallery. For good measure, he didn't wholly resemble Harvey Stone. Yet when he deliberately turned his head in profile there was no mistaking the nicked earlobe linking all three spectres.

Instinct told me he would flee however quickly I leaped up and bounded over the gravel paths and flowers beds. So instead I called out. "What do you *want* with me?"

He responded in a voice as unpleasantly fresh as when I'd first heard it over sixteen years earlier. "Got a drink on you? Price of a bottle?"

"Who *are* you?" I called out, standing up in my agitation. "How did you get that lump cut out of your ear?"

But his mind was on only one thing. "Chintzy bastard! Not even half a dollar, tightwad! Then what can you expect from pooftas!"

I sat back heavily on the stone bench and closed my eyes again. I knew, finally, that all attempts at communication were useless. As I expected, when I looked once more in his direction, there was just an empty seat. I was alone in the quiet garden.

The moment I met Ken at the foot of Buchanan Tower I greeted him with my fresh installment of the recurrent figure with the disfigured ear. He heard me out without interruption but then did a highly uncharacteristic thing. He put his arm firmly about my shoulders as faculty and students streamed alongside us, making for the parking lot behind Brock Hall.

"I don't think you'll see your drunken gent again. In fact I'm sure of it."

I stared at him in astonishment. "What on earth makes you say that? It's just started again after all that time."

"Before I taught my last class I got a phone call from Julius. His wife had asked him to call me. They heard last week that Harvey Stone had died.

I halted in the middle of the mall. "How?" I asked tersely.

"Suicide," Ken told me. "Lots of pills and lots of booze. The police found him in his apartment along Beach Avenue. His cleaning woman hadn't been able to get in." He gave me a queer little glance. "It was odd, you know. I'd scheduled a lecture on synchronicity in 19th century fiction. In the event I got a discussion going on something quite different in spite of my plans."

"I hope you're right about it not happening again," I said. "Sixteen or seventeen years of something like that is quite enough."

10

AN IMMIGRANT'S TALE

I met Stanlislaus Solski in the Gastown district of Vancouver — at a poetry meeting in a converted warehouse which had once been a garment factory. My diary tells me it was late November in 1972 and I distinctly recall him telling me soon after we had been introduced by Vera Maclean, that it happened to be his forty-third birthday. In that first spate of self-information he also informed me that he had an interest in writing although he was primarily a painter.

On learning that he was Polish I recognized such Slavic insignia as high cheekbones and his particularly straight hair which was brushed back from his forehead with no parting. His accent was so thick, his imperviousness to definite articles in his English so pronounced, that I was quite surprised to hear he had moved from Cracow to Montreal in the 1950s. He had been living in Vancouver only for the past year or so.

Comprehension — let alone conversation — was made even more difficult in that noisy room by the fact that he spoke quickly, with great emphasis, and was mightily concerned to impart as soon as possible a complete account of his beliefs, his accomplishments, and a welter of related matter. I decided to invite him for coffee in a nearby restaurant where it would be reasonably quiet and where I stood at least a chance of absorbing his torrent of words.

The café was at the corner of the block and while I hurried through a torrential downpour, my raincoat pulled hastily overhead, he continued to address me. By the time we sat down his blond hair was thoroughly flattened and his jacket darkened with damp. He was not deterred. He told me about the series of female nudes he'd just completed and then asked me if I knew of a suitable gallery he might approach. Even then I noticed he seemed more interested in the latter than the nude subjects. There was distinct scorn in his voice whenever he described his sitter. Nursing a white coffee mug between large hands he complained that his model never sat still enough. He laughed oddly then — as if at a secret joke. I didn't pick him up on it — he hardly gave me time — but I had the feeling that he wanted me to.

I noticed the paint smears on his denim shirt and that his fingernails were heavily engrimed as well as ochred from nicotine. In spite of his thickset shape he carried no surplus fat. I could see the lines of his ribs through the blue shirt.

"What do you do for a living?" I asked, when I could finally get a word in.

He shrugged, somehow conveying his contempt for the question. "I work poodle parlour for stoopid women with little dogs. No matter. I want gallery. What you think of New Design, eh?"

I prevaricated wildly. I had no inkling of what Stanislaus' work was like and wasn't going to make a commitment as to where he might show his canvasses. "Is this your first show? Have you had a *vernissage* in Vancouver before?" It was obvious the French term mean nothing to him. He ignored it.

"I not show nothinks till I ready. Now I ready. Thirty-three nudes I have. Some I calls spring, some summer, some fall and others winter. Background say which from which."

"Did you have a regular gallery in Montreal? You haven't told me anything about your training. Was that back in Poland? In Cracow?"

"I only sculptor then. Papier-mâché nudes — I do lots of them bastards. Now canvas, though. You know Bau-Xi gallery — if o.k.?"

"I should imagine the routine for you," I said carefully, "would be to take a few examples along and see what they feel at different places. If they like your work you can get down to financial arrangements."

He abruptly changed the subject. "Now we talk about writing. You writer, Vera says."

"Only in Englsh," I said quickly. "I don't know any Polish I'm afraid."

"I write now in English. Fiction and poems. I got lotsa poems — one fictions."

Hearing his English I could only shudder at the prospect of his written efforts. But I would have cut my throat rather than suggest my doubts. In the end, it was Stanislaus' vulnerability which had gotten through to me — not his deluge of words. I resolved then and there to do what I could for him.

The first thing, of course, was to see his paintings and I arranged before our hasty parting on the puddled sidewalk (where he still seemed inclined to remain talking) to visit him at his studio. This turned out to be his living room in a dialpidated building scheduled for demolition and thus rented at an extremely low rate from the city on the, then, still unfashionable Fairview slopes.

An old lady wearing a blue-spotted *babushka* above a black dress and looking very European, greeted me at the front door. Her lined face twisted into a smile revealing unnatural-looking dentures, as she learned who I was. Her accent was as guttural as that of Stanlislaus whom she identified as her son, but she had far fewer words at her disposal. "He expect. You come in."

I was ushered into a room off an uncarpeted corridor which was cramped by a bicycle propped against the wall, and a scratched baby carriage filled with sawn logs. The latter were obviously intended for the cast-iron stove that stood against the wall about midway down the large room which apparently stretched the length of the house. There were windows at each end but dirt and tattered curtains ensured a minimum of light. I gathered that Stanislaus, whose easel stood at the furthest end from where I'd entered, favored artificial light for his art.

The old lady vanished and I stood there awaiting the painter's arival. I wasn't surprised to see daubs of paint everywhere and to breathe an air redolent of oils, resin, and varnish. Yet there was more than the usual atmosphere of studio debris and untidiness with which I was relatively familiar as a free-lance art critic for various magazines. If there had been no easel, no evidences of a studio and the impedimenta of an artist's workplace, I would still have described the room as filthy. Combined with the odour of oil paint was the less pleasant one of stale sweat and — my immediately nervous nose insisted — of putrefaction. A dead mouse? Decomposing food?

I was left little time to debate the source. Stanislaus pushed past me from the hallway and almost ran over to what I could now make out was a pile of stacked canvases. "I show you all I got. Here, wanna sit?" He leaped across the room again to where a huge, plum-colored sofa, stacked with magazines and newspapers, stood in the window bay. Before I reached him he was sliding bundles of magazines to the floor and brushing the worn velour for me to sit down. Dust rose in clouds. I stopped in my tracks as my nose informed me that I was close to that cloyingly sweet smell of death. An accompanying whiff of urine convinced me that somewhere under all that junk lay a rotting mouse or rat. I wanted to gag. For relief I looked in the opposite direction towards the easel, hardly visible through the gloom. "I think I should move down further," I said firmly. "I can't see properly from this distance."

Stanislaus didn't falter in sliding National Geographics and other journals to the worn linoleum. "All change when I put on light. Not worry, Davey. You see like in gallery."

I wouldn't have sat down on the uncluttered space he had made unless he had physically forced me to do so. Nevertheless I just stubbornly stood there, my back to him, waiting for him to busy himself at the opposite end of his studio. He did prove to be right about the light, though. When he had fiddled with a couple of connections two spotlights on a ceiling crack flooded the easel and as he placed the first work up for me I had no difficulty whatever in seeing every detail of his work. Indeed, I had no difficulty in recognizing his model for the nude study. It was his mother. Only her eyes were closed in death and her wrinkled body lay with folded arms in the confines of a coffin lying in snow. Stanislaus made no comment, for once, but after throwing me a glance, exchanged the picture with another. The subject was once more his mother — only this time the recumbent figure lay on a tiled floor which was partially littered with sere brown leaves.

Every one of those thirty-three works depicted the old lady who had welcomed me at the front door! In each she was naked but none sported a common background. She was not always presented in a casket even if she invariably appeared dead. But her surround — just as he'd told me in the café — differed always in terms of the images the painter had used to suggest the four seasons. Frequently the frieze dominated the human subject at the center.

The execution of all these paintings was uniformly dreadful. It was only the obscene likeness to the old peasant woman I'd just met which imparted any power to them. They were very crude and not one of the canvases suggested innate talent. When the sequence was finally exhausted all I could find to mutter in response to his art was that I thought he had mastered death.

The process had lasted over an hour and I wasn't disposed to linger. He offered me coffee which I refused, but for the most part, as I backed desperately towards his front door and freedom, he followed me closely, babbling on in his broken English about the ugliness of the nude form and how important his backgrounds were! In the event, it was his old mother who, on rejoining us at the front door, asked the question which somehow he had skirted and which I most dreaded.

"You like Stanislaus art? You think good?"

I searched the currant eyes under the babushka. If she knew who was the subject of her son's nudes, she wasn't letting on. Instead, like him, she spoke about their setting. "Stanislaus good with winter, summer — them things. You feel hot or cold when you sees, no?"

"Yes indeed!!" I concurred, with dishonest vigor. "I think it's a marvellous idea!"

"Next I do stories like you. I fed up with painting women now." Stanislaus spoke forcibly over his mother's diminutive shoulder.

"I really have to go. I'm already late for my next appointment," I lied.

"Here, Davey. You look at these, eh?" From behind his back Stanislaus magically produced a substantial sheaf of papers and I covertly groaned at their quantity. "This my fiction I told you in café? I write in English but it need cleanin' up. You help there I think."

I thought otherwise, but I took the bundle from him all the same. As I backed slowly down the rickety steps of the house I grimaced in false response to the smiling little woman who seemed almost a dwarf, framed there in the portal, jammed against her son who was also grinning and thus exposing his bad teeth, as they both waved me goodbye.

Confession time. It was only after one whole week and two phone calls from Stanislaus that I finally forced myself to read his grubby manuscript. It gave the impression of having been already read by every publisher in Canada, and a goodly number south of the border, before being thrust into my own reluctant hands.

That said, I have to admit that his narrative impressed me. The lurid evocation of a flat and desolate terrain east of the Elbe was oddly strengthened by the writer's idiosyncratic English. It gave it a powerful autobiographic sense. The result was that the sheer intensity of his clumsy account of a boy's fleeing first from Germans, then Russians, held me to page after page — even when my eyes blurred with fatigue as I lay in bed.

When I had finished reading Stanislaus' manuscript I was faced with a double dilemma. Given my reactions to his paintings I could not possibly recommend them to such as Paul Wong at the Bau Xi, or the other galleries in town. And as much as I was impressed by his writing, I remained convinced it needed some major overhauling before a publisher would take it seriously.

This was my solution. I told Stanislaus that he should try a gallery co-operative of young artists for an exhibition and I also suggested he join me and a small group of writers who met regularly to read their work to each other and then discuss it. I took care to stress that we didn't allow our gatherings to degenerate into bloodbaths of critical attack and that I felt he would be warmly welcomed by my friends and could benefit substantially from their subsequent remarks.

He did secure an exhibition for himself at the Co-op, although there was no critical coverage I heard of. I also had the impression he never sold a single work. I didn't attend the show and Stanislaus never made further reference to it. In fact he hardly mentioned his paintings again to me. His writing had become the dominant theme between us.

Although I took good care not to accept any of his requests to return to his place for coffee and chat, we did start to meet with some regularity at an expresso bar on Fourth Avenue in Kitsilano. I think he particularly took to the place as there were still signs of vestigial 'hippydom' in sartorial evidence. On those rare occasions he seemed aware of external circumstance, as he sat there hunched over his glass cup, he would express satisfaction with the long hair, the fronded leather, and the occasional onkh adorning the necks of either gender.

There was one overwhelming consistency to Stanislaus' mien: his intensity. But it served violently disparate moods. When he was depressed and disconsolate, he was usually brimming with suspicion that most of those whom he knew, especially the women, were malevolent in intent. In vain did I seek to persuade him that Canadians, the Anglo-Saxons at least, were generally stingy in praise and loathe to articulate their appreciation of human worth or endeavor. In vain, also, did I try to convince him that British Columbia was neither the Balkans nor Eastern Europe; that all his allusions to machination and plot were figments of his imagination and that a failure to wave a hand in acknowledgement on the street or to warmly address him at the poodle parlor didn't necessarily mean a rebuke or slight.

When he was feeling cheerful, not only was the psychic energy unabated, but the rhetoric of his self-confidence disturbed me as much as his paranoia when his mood was black. I cringed when he spoke of his manuscript. *The Uprooting*, as "my masterpiece which will shake world" and donated to that and the short stories on which he had now embarked, a similar hyperbole to that he had previously accorded those now unmentioned canvases which I assumed lay piled up against each other in the murk of that evil-smelling room.

I shall not quickly forget the time we sat in La Bocca Café and Stanislaus (allowing his expresso to grow cold and its bubbles to subside) with glittering eyes and loud voice joshed me in a manner I'm sure he thought both good-humored and well-intentioned.

"Ah, Davey, you and your bourgeois friends I about to meet — you all die of shock when book come out. You all writes silly little stuff about your love affairs, no? Ignore big world I come from. What any of you know about hunger and rape, eh? I see it all. One day you and group say you proud to know Stanislaus Solski. You see! Solski Nobel Prize wins! First Canadian in world, eh?" He was laughing and I knew that even he was aware of his extreme language. But I also sensed the underlying seriousness. For that never deserted my friend; even in sleep I suspected.

Thus I often returned home after these volatile encounters troubled for someone so demanding of life. I even debated whether I wanted to see him again — at least in a one-to-one context. The solution seemed to be our literary meetings where I could take refuge in numbers. The trouble with that, though, was that we usually met monthly and Stanislaus was not the kind of man to live on any sort of mensal basis.

I am skirting a further reality: my own disposition. True, there were the times when I told myself vehemently that people like Stanislaus had a fiendish ability to suck one down into the vortex of their own despair and leave one exhausted — while they walked away on springy toe, ready to drain the very next person they met! But I couldn't gainsay my fascination with the man. There was little of physical attraction but my bemusement with the whole gamut of his extravagant emotions and cosmic gestures certainly extended beyond my quite genuine conviction that *The Uprooting* was the work of a talented artist. So we continued to meet, intermittently, over coffee in public places where I usually sat silent save for the occasional (and quite superfluous!) prompting, while he thundered on about shaping masterpieces from the jetsam of his past.

The irony of it all was that while for me these encounters proved most depleting, it was the literary meetings — when he had a chance to show off his writing and receive positive comment on it — which evoked his acute displeasure and brought him pain. Each of these distressing occasions involved women.

Here, I think, I should indicate the composition of our group. We were six or seven in all but it was rare for more than five to turn up at one session. The regulars, apart from myself, were Constance Fisher, a nurse at St. Paul's Hospital, Doug McIntyre, a C.B.C. Radio producer, Mary Brandreth, an Instructor in the English Department at U.B.C., and Saul Cohen, a colleague of Mary's at the university.

We three men Stanislaus more or less ignored at these meetings but he took an immediate interest in both women — an interest which manifestly had little or nothing to do with their literary prowess. He always sat next to a woman if it proved possible when we were assembled in the living room of one or other of us, and squatted on the floor between Mary and Constance whenever the chance presented itself.

When it was a male's turn to read from his work, I noted with growing irritation, that our new member either scanned his own pages or clumsily flirted with a female neighbor. Usually his callow comments were ignored but if he actually succeeded in impeding a reading there was a chorused hiss of anger and he was told sharply to shut up. But even if he did it was only for the briefest period. Otherwise he retreated into silence which could last throughout a meeting. At the third such gathering involving him he fastened his attention upon Constance and that generated the first exchange of irate words I'd ever encountered since first attending the sessions over two years earlier. Stanislaus was sprawled upon a large yellow pillow on the living-room floor of Doug's West End apartment. Constance was ensconced on a leather, steel-tubed chair as she read from a collection of poems scheduled to appear the following year. In many respects Constance was our 'senior' participant, not so much in years but because she was a founder-member of the group and had published her stuff with fair regularity since her student days in Victoria.

She had come straight from the hospital and had not changed out of her nurse's uniform. She had rather a deep voice and, although it could be monotonous, the timbre particularly suited the verses she was reading which were concerned with seabirds and loneliness on the reaches of Long Beach along the westcoast of Vancouver Island.

Suddenly Stanislaus bent his head nearly to the floor and started to intone, in competition with her rendition of the poem, the doggerel lines of childhood: "I see England, I see France, I see someone's underpants."

The contralto voice stopped abruptly. There was silence in the room where the five of us sat in semi-circle. "Don't be an idiot," Constance finally ground out over our embarassment. "We don't go in for that kind of crap — anymore than I would take it from my male patients. Davey should've told you."

I felt the implied accusation unfair and said as much. "I'm hardly responsible for a member's manners," I told her hotly. "I assume politeness, just as we all do surely."

"You look good angry," Stanislaus said, grinning at Constance and eyeing her up and down in a thoroughly lewd way. "You better when not bullshitting and reading all that bird crap."

"For Chrissakes, grow up," the lady told him, "or aren't you used to being around adults? I've heard about Polish jokes, of course, but this is the first time I've ever had to meet one."

Amazingly, Stanislaus shut up at that. But I noticed how his face reddened and how white spots appeared on both cheeks. That would not prove the end of the incident, I told myself, and sadly I was proved right. When it came time for Saul Cohen to read us his story, Stanislaus again grew restless. Perhaps he intended the remark to be delivered *sotto voce* but I don't think so. "Now more shit about them spoiled-rotten students and middle class life, eh?"

Doug McIntyre, as apartment lender and in concert with our general practice, now acted as spokesman and group-leader. "It's our custom to be quiet when others are reading, so please belt up, Stanislaus. Just as we did when we listened to your stuff. It's the only way these groups work, I assure you. Then perhaps you never got a chance to discover such things."

For a moment I thought Stanislaus was going to walk out on us. I need not have worried. I recalled that he was never enthusiastic about public transportation and that I had picked him up as usual and driven him there. He was sullenly silent throughout the rest of the meeting and remained so in the car afterwards, not even returning my 'goodnight' when he shot out of the Peugeot and hurried up his rickety steps without looking back. Before the group met again, of course, there were lengthy phone discussions as to whether Stanislaus should be allowed further participation. Constance, oddly enough, did not side with the majority. She emphasized the fact that as a newcomer, he still had to acustom himself to our ways — ways, which she stressed, had codified and grown more intricate as time had passed. Mary Brandreth then wondered if he always understood us when we spoke so rapidly in English. I assured her that he did but she persisted in referring to his thick Polish accent and didn't sound convinced. Saul Cohen, whose relationship with Mary was prickly at best, disagreed with her. He said they had enough colleagues on campus with heavy accents which in no way impeded their plotting and participating in departmental intrigue. The rest of us were united in expressing our disapproval of his conduct and insisted that if he continued in the future, he had to be dropped. However, the final conclusion was that he should be given a last chance.

At the next meeting which was held in my place in Kitsilano, it was my turn to read, along with Doug. Everything went smoothly at first, even though yet again Stanislaus had inserted himself on the sofa between Mary and Constance. This time it was Mary he was to rile.

The readings over, it was now refreshment time and private chit-chat prevailed. Marty, between sips at her tea-mug, was talking to me about my story of a Russian Archimandrite living in Paris and his mischievous ways. In the course of my recitation Stanislaus had sighingly demonstrated his boredom with my fiction. Now Mary, in slightly turning her back on him to address me more effectively, added to his displeasure. He had frequently informed me of his antipathy towards anything Russian but even more frequently had he railed against being snubbed or ignored, most particularly by a woman.

Our prickly Pole now found himself with the alternatives of Mary's impervious shoulder or a Constance whom he had steadfastly ignored all evening and who, in any case, was now preoccupied with a Saul Cohen who was anxious for her to examine an inflamed eye and diagnose it for him.

I had just relaxed back at the far end of the sofa (the left foot of my crossed legs twitching with satisfaction at the unexpected praise of acerbic Mary) when, from the corner of my eye, I saw Stanislaus deliberately tip his coffee mug so that some of its contents spilled down on the thighs of his neighbor. Queen Victoria's oft-remarked failure to be amused was as nothing compared to Mary's reaction.

"What the fuck! You did that on purpose, you bastard! You dumb Polish sonofabitch!"

The rest of us said nothing: quelled by her ferocity. She was never what one might call genteel but neither did she normally cuss with such abandon. (Then neither was scalding customary at our get-togethers.) Only Stanlislaus seemed unperturbed. He just grinned at her. "You got big ass," he told her through those uneven yellow teeth. "You take too much room on sofa."

I saw her hand leap up from her coffee-soaked jeans and the mug he still held poised above her legs, go hurtling through the air towards the window bay. What I didn't see — though I certainly heard — was her follow-up with a sharp smack across his mouth. As his head jerked back on the sofa I could observe the dribble of blood which the blow brought to the side of his now closed lips.

After that everything seemed to happen in slow motion. From the other side of him Constance turned from Saul and addressed him icily. "I defended your stupid behavior once but I'll not do it again. I saw you do that and it was unforgiveable. They were right and I was wrong. You're a pig. I guess you always will be a damn pig. You obviously don't belong here," she continued in her deep voice. "Davey," she said, leaning forward, "tell him to leave your house."

I was mustering up courage to do just that when Stanislaus forestalled me. At least, he got heavily to his feet, wiping his mouth roughly so that the blood smeared. Instead of turning towards the door he faced the two women still sitting on the sofa. They both stared up at him angrily — although their expression swiftly changed as he very deliberately unzipped his pants, withdrew his penis, and waved it just inches from their faces.

I couldn't help noticing that he was amply endowed but that thought was quickly dislodged by the bizarre notion that he was about to urinate on them. I sensed Doug move from my other side but before he could reach the middle portion of the sofa, the offending Stanislaus had made it quite clear that his intention was not to humiliate but to taunt them. His voice was oddly shrill. "This is what you bitches want! All you want the same! I see it in Poland when you take from me. Old witches hold me down and they take what they want. I just kid but I learn fast!" He abruptly wagged his cock in the direction of Mary's nose. "Here, bitch, take this, eh? You talk all academic shit but this what you want. I knows." Then he pointed it at tight-lipped Constance. "What you nurses do to mens, eh? I have that in Europe, too. When I in camp with bust arm and all them bandages, nurses play with me like fucking puppy dog! I knows what you do men in hospital when they can't do nothings. Hell, I offer free when I not all bound up and dizzy on them drugs you always giving mens in beds."

As quickly as he he had pulled out his cock he returned it to his trousers. By now Doug was at his side, tugging him away from the sofa and the women. I saw controlled fury envelop him as Doug laid hands upon him. With a savage downthrust he brushed the producer's timid efforts at restraint away, turned, and strode towards the living room door.

He stood at the threshhold for a moment, struggling I think for some final words of abuse to encompass us all. But he merely mouthed silently. I had time to notice that he still hadn't zipped up his fly before he passed from our sight.

We had a postmortem of sorts about his outlandish behavior, but it was strained and soon fizzled out before my guests went home. It was at our next literary group meeting that Constance informed us she had learned that Stanislaus had been committed to Riverview after being charged in Kerrisdale with attempted rape.

In the course of our discussion I reluctantly volunteered to visit him in that grim complex along the Fraser Valley but Constance advised me not to. She had a friend there and he had told her that apart from Stanislaus not wishing to receive any visitors save his mother, he was suffering memory loss and in all likelihood wouldn't know who I was. I was secretly glad to be let off the hook as somehow he had filled me with a guilt which until now has been as private as it has persistently refused to go away. I still lie awake some nights thinking of our Polish victim and the strange heritage of his ills.

——11——

IT TAKES ONE TO KNOW ONE

You see a great deal from the lanes in Vancouver. The streets themselves, more often than not, offer only closed faces. Drapes conceal window eyes and what lies behind them. Solid doors stopper the mouths of houses and in Kitsilano where Carolyn Carr lived in 1973 (the year of the streaker during the Academy Awards) tall hedges of bamboo, or laurel frequently hid such treasures of westcoast spring as blood-red camelias or the vibrant tangerine of particularly splendid azaleas.

At first Carolyn was just an immense female shape whom I estimated to be in her early seventies who carted her garbage cans out behind her garage on Mondays. She was usually followed by a diminutive figure carrying supplementary bundles of waste she referred to as simply 'Carr' and whom I correctly took to be her husband. She ignored me as I walked the dogs past her — then her attention was more than taken up by the little man with a white frieze about his bald head who wheezed and coughed from what sounded unpleasantly like emphysema as he followed behind her with his lesser load wrapped in a plastic bag.

Carolyn did not speak to me — and thus I did not learn her name — until spring had moved on from bulbs and the first flowering shrubs into orange scented syringa and the first rosebuds. I was taking the dogs for a walk in Tatlow Park and Carolyn caught me as I illicitly encouraged them to defecate by the roots of a giant cedar.

"That's a good place for 'em to shit," she observed as I embarrassedly prayed they would straighten their humped backs, scratch back feet into the needled soil and behave as if nothing had happened before more hostile eyes chanced upon us. Carolyn's fence bordered the park and it was over this that she leaned as we engaged in our very first conversation. It was then I learned that 'Carr' was also Sydney and that the two of them had been married over forty years and that both were natives of the city of Liverpool and had emigrated to Canada, to Vancouver, soon after World War Two.

If I hadn't guessed Liverpool I would most certainly have opined the north of England for Carolyn Carr had brought an accent intact with her and had lost none of it during the subsequent years. That was not all she had brought. There was, for instance that hair net she wore like a wartime 'snood' which not only flattened her grey-brown locks until they appeared perpetually sodden from the rain, but allowed her to wear the most incongruous and odd bangs which made her look even more emphatically English, even if I cannot say why, exactly.

When looking down over that fence at me I really saw for the first time how plain she was. Her nose was as coarse as her face was puffy. All that could be said in its favour was it congruously matched the bulk of her body.

It was only what one could perceive of the eyes, embedded as they were in the puffy flesh, that suggested a measure of intelligence. And here again, the unsympathetic could easily have invoked the word crafty to describe those cold grey objects which darted incessantly in the act of appraisal and judgement.

"What kind of dog is that," she asked.

"A standard poodle," I told her.

"Thought as much. We had one of them back there. Only he was white. Came from the Duke of Carlisle's kennels. His Grace give it to us when we was during a job for him."

I didn't have a clue as to what she was talking about. I was just thinking of how proud I was of Max. He really was a superb black poodle. I looked next at Simon, our little fawn pug — and wondered whether Carolyn might say something nice about him, too. But it was evidently Max who had caught her fancy. "White, all of 'em was. Then the Duke only liked white. It was always the same. Herd of wild white cattle — priceless they was. Then the fleet of Rolls they was all white too. That's where we come in, of course. Carr and I serviced the whole bloody lot. Used to drive up from Liverpool — bombs or no bombs — and go over 'em from top to bottom. Sometimes I had all six to do on me own of course. Like when Carr was off on a special job. It was only later I joined up with my husband in that special stuff. That's when the poor old Rolls had to take second place up there on the estate.

I was still only half listening to her as Simon obviously felt like an extensive dig among the roots beneath the cedar needles.

"Special job?" I queried. "What kind of special job? With Rolls Royces?"

She smiled in almost coy fashion. "Not really. Though it's true that by the end of the war Sidney Carr and his wife, Carolyn, were the firm's top trouble shooters. That's what they called us, all over England. Next stop would have been here if we hadn't called it off and decided we needed a rest. But the special, dear was quite different. Hush-hush even now, if you don't mind."

That sounded so ridiculous I felt embarrassed. I changed the subject. "I ought to take the dogs around Tatlow Park," I told her.

I read disappointment in her face so I wasn't really surprised when she came up with an invitation. "Why don't you drop by when you're through? Carr would like to see the dogs. The poodle will take him down memory lane. He needs taking out of himself, does Sidney Carr."

She spoke of her husband but it did not conceal the personal plea. I told her I'd stop by on my way home and would be grateful for the coffee which she offered.

That time I entered the Carr's home remains an indelible memory. Nothing to do with the small house or its furnishings. They were ordinary enough in a petit bourgeois fashion. That's to say with the plastic ducks across the wall behind the green sofa with its goldwire motif, the large mirror behind the mantelpiece and the clock with the Westminster chimes dead center between the crowded bric-a-brac. No, all such minor aesthetic irritation blurred to irrelevance in the face of the Carr's marital teamwork. I had never seen anything quite like it. It wasn't just the feeding of him lines and the sense of rehearsed ease as they covered their heroic exploits during WW2 and after. It was equally the incredible smoothness of collaboration that seduced me into an awed admiration and a salute to a domestic theatre of a calibre I had never previously witnessed.

Sidney Carr had the somewhat pompous mien of a number of short men. He sat with his patent-black shoes just off the carpet — the chair being slightly too high for him. He held his hands together, palm to palm, his tapering fingers extended as if in prayer and propping up his chin as he made a pedantic point or yet another arcane allusion to their wartime exploits. Sitting opposite to him Carolyn filled mugs with Nescafé and passed them over to us while the electric kettle on its cord from the kitchen hissed on the acrylic carpet by her side. "Tell him, Carr, about the N5 caper. He'd appreciate that being a dog-lover and all."

"Come on old girl, button up now. O.S.A. and all that. You understand, Son. *Official Secrets Act?* We're still tied, you know. Still got to padlock the old tongue! But them big poodles was something again. Old Royce, you know, loved his poodles. That's why the space between the back seat and the partition in a Rolls Royce exactly fits the standard poodle's proportions. Do you know that I reached the state of audio perfection with the Rolls motor? I could tell if she was in perfect tune at a radius of 2,000 metres?"

"So could I, Carr, so could I. Don't forget the Worthington incident! If it hadn't been for Carolyn Carr there wouldn't have been a single tank from our chaps on the Eastern Front. Then where would they have been, eh? No Stalingrad, no Murmansk, nothing if you ask me!"

"Our friend here doesn't want to hear about Ruskie ingratitude, lass. He's too young. Let bygones be bygones — that's the password of this generation. Dogs, isn't it lad?" He looked across at his spouse who was scowling slightly below her bangs. "Did you know there was a time when Mrs. Carr and I were responsible for importing over three hundred Norwegian Elkhounds to northern Greenland?" He did not await an answer. "It was part of the canine miscegnation plan I dreamed up for the Danish government. They'd approached Sir Rolls..."

"You mean Sir Henry, surely, Carr."

"I mean Sir Royce, of course. They'd approached Sir Henry and he'd just dumped the whole thing in my lap as usual and said 'this is something I can safely leave to you and yours, Sid. You've never let the firm down in the past and I cannot see you doing so now.' The point you've got to remember, Son, is that in them days Greenland belonged to Denmark and there was a certain amount of frothin' friction between the two. I might go as far as to say that the lives of Mrs. C and Yours Truly were in danger from time to time."

"Really," I blurted, unable to suppress sarcastic surprise for a moment more. "From the dogs I suppose. They were that hungry?"

Like the Mississippi, Ole Man Carr just kept rolling. He was undivertable. "Miscegenation means the inter-breeding of distinct species or sub-species. In Greenland they was having a lot of trouble with timber wolves. Our plan was to introduce those fierce creatures to the docile Norwegian Elkhound and via mating activities modify the volpine ferocity and thus come up with a gentler wolf."

Carolyn too her cue immediately from him. "In order to effect this result it was decided that I would hold our bitches when they were in heat and await the arrival of the male wolves when they were attracted by the females. My task was to grab the bitch until the coupling was effected — then we could be certain of union for our written report."

"Unfortunately," her husband continued, "the wolves were hostile to our personal involvement and even in the act of copulation would bite my better half when she was merely trying to assist. She spent most of her time getting stitched up in Thule, didn't you, Lass? Show him your scars, why don't you?"

As if on cue Carolyn Carr whipped up her skirt with one hand and brandished her arm at one and the same time. It was all so quick that I really had time only to notice blue veins standing out from mottled white flesh but I was more than ready to take their word for her Greenland legacy.

"It must have been very unpleasant," I interjected. "Tell me, do you find life in Canada a bit of an anti-climax after all your adventures." I looked from one to the other, not caring who spoke but anxious to have the sight of ancient flesh removed from my vision.

With obvious reluctance, Carolyn let the folds of her skirt fall and tugged at the sleeve of her loose-fitting cardigan. Her husband spoke. "Between you, me and the gate-post, Son, it's a bloody bore! Now I find myself listening on Monday mornings for the sound of the garbage truck. Do you know what Mondays *used* to mean?"

Carolyn leaned forward, still disgruntled I felt. "Tell him, Carr. Tell him just what Mondays used to mean."

I tried to look at my wrist watch from the corner of my eye but failed. They were both scrutinizing me to perceive the effect of Sidney Carr's next revelation.

"Tell me about Mondays," I said, surrendering.

"Mondays we received orders, my boy. The boss had a short-wave receiver and transmitter installed in our personal Rolls and at eleven a.m., never fail, the instructions would come over the set. 'You are due in Shanghai in five days' ... 'In ten days you will be deep-sea diving off the coast of Labrador' ... 'Be prepared to meet potentates tonight. Formal dress and medals to be worn' ... 'Carry firearms in case of emergency'..."

Sidney's eyes glazed in memory and he tailed off. But Carolyn promptly took over. "...'get down to Holloway Prison in London. You will meet an inmate who will smuggle you a package' ... Every Monday," she added breathlessly, "would see us off at some time to some place. Nine times out of ten Sid would be sitting behind the wheel of our purring Rolls while I sat next to him with the maps and the compass out."

Her husband seemed to make an effort to break out of the spell of reverie. "Mind you," he said slowly, "sometimes we was off to check another Rolls that had developed trouble. We were the chief United Kingdom trouble-shooters, like the Missus told you."

"How fascinating," I said, politely but, I hoped, with finality. "I could sit and listen for hours. But these chaps are getting restless," I explained, pointing down to the two dogs who were sitting perfectly happily at my feet. "It's their dinnertime," I fibbed.

"But we haven't told you about the sabotage in the Duke's kennels." They spoke in unison for the first time. I was impressed. Nevertheless, I got to my feet which did make the dogs stir. "I'd love to hear, *next* time," I said. "We've said nothing about his white poodles," they chorused, "nothing about the wild white cattle and how we saved the Royal Liver Building from arson with a bicycle pump."

"Let that be first on the agenda," I told them as I bent and affixed leashes on the collars of both dogs. "But next time."

As I made for the door they fell silent. Neither of them moved to show me the way out. Sidney seemed vanquished, appeared smaller than ever as he sat there, bald head shrunk further between hunched shoulders like an ailing bird. She ceased to dart her eyes but batted them instead. Her iron grey bangs no longer fell evenly across her coarse forehead and her bulges squashed into the sister armchair to the one I'd vacated, heaved up and down as if she was stoking up for a cry. I felt compassion for the poor old thing, even if my determination to get out of that place was now as tough as flint. "I'll give a shout when I bring the dogs up next to Tatlow," I muttered. "Maybe we can take a turn through the park together."

I had pushed the backdoor open before she answered. And then her voice was listless, the flat vowels of her Liverpudlian accent strangely subdued. "Doubt it, Lad. I doubt it. Carr don't go out any more — and they never come back, do they Sid?"

Now that my feet were actually on the threshhold I paused: briefly irresolute. Besides, I was reluctant to shut the door behind me. It seemed vaguely impertinent on my part. The hiatus permitted me to hear her husband's reply.

"Let him go, Lass. He were only half listening anyways. I were watching his feet and they never stopped wiggling. I reckon they're all the same — it's a selfish generation nowadays."

I carefully closed the door behind me so that it didn't even click. Back out there in the lane I unleashed the dogs and raced the two of them home. Max won of course, and for the last few yards I grabbed Simon the pug and ran with him squirming in my arms. It took my mind off the Carrs.

* * *

In September, two days after the rain-drenched Labor Day, Jimmy McGuire asked me to his West End apartment to meet a mysterious guest. Jimmy is one of a small Vancouver group which might be described as the scions of wealthy and comparatively affluent social families. His had been involved in small time manufacturing for the forest industry in the early 1900s, sold out to a major American firm and lived off the proceeds, with a bit of investing, for the next fifty years. Jimmy had never worked and although he had taken a nightclass I'd given at Kitsilano High School on Northwest painters, I'd soon realized it had been only in a dilettantish fashion and that it was just another way of filling an evening in a rather empty succession of them. Jimmy had but one hobby — collecting people, especially people who shared his passion for trivia concerning the Royal Family and some knowledge of both British and European aristocracy and one's own bloodlines. Jimmy, in fact, was an amiable snob and talk at his dinner table I often felt was more suitable for the paddock at a thoroughbred racing stable than for a non-equine congregation. Nevertheless he was an attractive, warm-hearted man in his early thirties, served excellent food and never stinted on his wines. I rarely refused his invitations.

I suppose the kind of information I have just recorded should have led me to suspect something about his dinner-guest whom he merely hinted was a woman, and a distinguished academic. But I didn't. When I stood in the elevator with a fellow guest, Connie van der Hoof (one of Jimmy's oldest friends), we both tried to guess who the guest of honor might prove to be. Connie, whose father was a judge and vaguely related to our host's mother, took off her gaberdine raincoat, shook the raindrops all over the elevator which included me, and suggested that Guest X was probably Queen Marie of Roumania. "He's been reading a book about her and Jimmy loves to follow things up whenever possible."

We had reached the penthouse and our chatter came to an end. For the first few moments, on entering the apartment, I forgot guests and concentrated on that magnificent view. The earlier rain had washed the atmosphere in that unique westcoast fashion which bequeaths a legacy of such exceptional brilliance and clarity that distances are wiped out and the northshore mountains appear to have half-crossed English Bay and narrowed the sea. The contrasting blues of water and sky were also thrust forward in prominence by the rugged jet contours of the mountain peaks beyond which a late summer sun afforded the first hint of dying.

The noisy traffic on Beach Avenue far below didn't disturb us, so comfortably ensconced in Jimmy's luxurious eagle's nest. With difficulty, I turned from the plate glass window where the evening star struggled to twinkle through a too bright daylight blue. The living room brimmed with taste. Unfortunately the taste was not mine. True, there was an elegant bird charcoal by Morris Graves on one wall facing a large and triumphant Gordon Smith acrylic opposite. But the enormous glass coffee table, the sea of biscuit carpet into which one sank up to the ankles, the tubular steel armchairs and the general air of Italian opulence smacked of interior decorator chic; the GQ and the Architectural Quarterly. I only really felt comfortable in that place when sitting at the grey oak dining table with my bottom resting on the pale green leather of tall backed chairs that were custom-made for Jimmy by an Austrian craftsman in New Westminster. Then Jimmy is a first-rate cook and spares no expense on his victuals.

The meal was at least an hour away as Connie urged me to join her on the cushion-littered sofa and Jimmy came back from the kitchen with the martinis we both requested. Across from us, on a black leather loveseat, sat Robert Martin, whose claim to fame lay dually in his Haida Indian blood and the fact he was the most expensive landscape gardener in the city. I was about to josh him about a ridiculous photograph of him and his Airdale bitch, Star, when all four of us were distracted by a doorbell rung not once, not twice but several times. I looked at my neighbor and grinned. The newcomer whom I presumed to be Jimmy's mystery guest, was determined to make a grand entrance.

We were left little time for comment or composure as even before Jimmy could reach the front door it flung open to admit a diminutive woman dressed largely in black including a large-brimmed hat with a veil attached. Her perfume reached us before she did. As we were all introduced I noted with pleasure the attractiveness of her French-accented speech. It was both husky and contralto deep. Her English, though, was most assured and, I was to learn shortly after, the peer of anyone in that expanse of penthouse living room.

At first, though, Monique Marie Benoit was not the most audible person present. Connie and Robert Martin fell into one of their City Hall routines where he brilliantly sent up Harry Makin, a pugnacious Alderman whose passion for rhetoric was umatched by his verbal resources and Connie gave us Iris Creek, a relative newcomer to the Council scene who although born on the anonymous slopes of South Vancouver, believed that a Southern Belle approach was the most effective to solve problems ranging from sewage processes to the blatant nudity of Wreck Beach.

Whether it was ignorance of such subject matter, antipathy for it, or a combination of both, Connie's and Robert's banter was soon lanced by Monique-Marie who suddenly addressed me from the far end of the long sofa where she sat in comparative isolation. "The last time I was publicly nude I was looking down the barrel of a Gestapo officer's revolver," she said with a thin smile.

"Was it summer or winter?" I enquired sweetly. "Gun metal can be so cold to the skin, can't it?" I thought, of course, that she was kidding.

Lesson number one with Monique-Marie Benoit — she *never* kidded, especially over autobiography.

I don't think the others heard our little exchange for they continued to offer the company a Harry Makin in full tirade against turds on sidewalk and city parks and his adversary on council, Iris Creek, addressing the same topic through the delicate euphenism of 'winter crocuses', which she defended as the small price tag of Man's Best Friend.

Monique, though, had not finished with me, let alone with her adventures in frontal nudity and the German secret police. "It was mid-winter," she explained patiently, her voice quite expressionless. "Otherwise little Patrice would not have died. There were five naked children as well as me, their aunt, standing in the castle courtyard in the freezing wind while those German pigs threatened our lives and made obscene gestures with their firearms and truncheons."

"I'm sorry — I had no idea," I began. "You look so young. I never dreamed that the war could have involved someone like you."

She nodded sympathetically, graciously accepting my embarrassed apologies. "I was barely sixteen. Not much more than a child. But my brother was head of the Resistance for the whole of Savoie. They hated him enough to take a photograph of my two nephews and nieces before torturing them, and another of me in the nude which they pinned to the corpse of Patrice and left in the market square of St. Martin where they knew the Freedom Fighters would discover it."

By now the amateur vaudeville team had fallen silent. Host Jimmy was staring bug-eyed as he listened to further dramatic tales of Monique's adventures in wartime France under the Ocupation. Many of her anecdotes concluded on a rather self-denigratory note which she would accompany with a slight lowering of her head and sometimes a biting of her lower lip as if caught in embarassment at the girlish innocence which had led her initially into peril, or her feminine frailty when she had failed to cut a ship's painter in time, or only stunned some Gestapo thug when she had intended to kill.

It was precisely after she had described such an aborted murder that Jimmy hastily suggested we have dinner. We were soon to learn that neither food nor an excellent '59 Beaune was about to deflect the lady who sat at her host's right and continued to regale the four of us with her remarkable exploits. True, between the coquille St. Jacques which was accompanied with a beguiling *Puilly Fuissée* and the fashionable rack of Salt Spring lamb and the aforementioned burgundy, we were treated to a diversion by Monique when she told us of her experiences as a tutor to several youthful members of the British Royal Family. This had come about, I gathered (although my mind might well have wandered and my appreciation of precise fact faltered) through Monique's distant sanguinary connection with the Greek Royals and thus with Prince Philip. In any event she seemed to have had relaxed and frequent encounters with numerous exalted personnages and to have stayed not only at Balmoral and Windsor but in half the stately homes of England. Nor were her sorties confined to the blood royal. She spoke of 10 Downing Street as if it were her local pub and of prime ministers, lords of commerce and industry and members of both Houses of Parliament, as the bread and butter of her social life. Long before the Baked Alaska the rest of us had looked at each other with a smile, secretly hoping, I suspect, that by her loquacious presence among us she was implicitly stating our equality with the exalted types she had left behind during her teaching and tutoring period in the United Kingdom. That, indeed, was the kind of weird gratitude she was oddly able to confer. There were times when I felt my credulity jarred by the excesses of her anecdote; but the next minute I was flattered by her intimacy and her gift of speaking of the famous without for a moment providing an irritating sense she was merely dropping names.

But I began to perceive that she was only truly at ease when she was in charge — conversationally speaking. So that when Connie suddenly asked Jimmy if he had finished Queen Marie of Rumania as she'd like to read the biography herself, our French guest turned again to me and reverted to the subject of her wartime adventures as a young girl. "I only met Queen Marie once," she said, "and that wasn't in the pleasantest circumstances. It was at a funeral in the Russian Orthodox Cathedral on the rue Darue. It was a Requiem for the Archbishop and it was obvious that the embalming hadn't taken on the old man. Queen Marie offered me some extra strong peppermints as I joined her in paying respects at the bier. I must say even all the incense the Orthodox use wasn't enough to conceal the putrefaction."

I was glad there was no food on my plate at that moment. But it was something else which prevented me just following her gaily delivered words. I had a nagging sense that I had heard what she was saying before. However hard I strained in mental recollection I could not think of where or when. But as minute followed minute and her brilliantly evoked story received further lively embellishment, I grew ever more convinced that I had learned it all elsewhere. Then I looked at Jimmy. He, too, I could see by the puzzled expression he wore, had similar thoughts to mine buzzing through his curly head. When Monique drew breath, he said as much. "Didn't that happen to Queen Mary? I mean at the funeral of Czar Alexander."

This, Monique dismissed airily. "I am sure it has been commonplace at these large state funerals where the corpse has to be kept until all the visitors have arrived. But in any case, dear Jimmy, even you must realise that Czar Alexander was somewhat before my time. Do I really look that old?" She smile demurely and looked supplicatingly up and down the table. There was a dutiful chorus of denial. The serpent of doubt may have crept into that dining room but gallantry had not departed.

In the resulting shift in mood and the splutter of general conversation which now erupted, our host proposed we remove to the living room for coffee and liqueurs. I was struck by the alacrity of my fellow guests in carrying out his suggestion. Connie nudged me as we left the table. "Now we can get down to some decent gossip and get away from World War Two and royalty," she whispered. "I've never felt such a pacifist republican as tonight."

"Don't be bitchy," I scolded, "she's just nervous and feeling her way with us."

My companion shrugged. Even I was taken aback when she responded so coldly. "Where the hell does Jimmy find them," she exclaimed. "Remember the Oakalla number who stole half the apartment before heading east with his parole officer at his heels?"

"You're too harsh," I said. And added just because I knew it would annoy her, "You wouldn't be so hostile if she weren't a woman, and an attractive one at that."

The exchange was aborted by Monique herself. She took my arm as we entered the hallway. Connie immediately left my other side and headed for the bathroom. "We haven't really had a chance to chat. Jimmy says you were born in Cornwall and educated in France?"

"Yes to the Cornwall bit but France needs some modification. And you? Born in Beaune, did I hear you say? Then you seem to have spent a lot of time in Britain as well."

To my mild surprise she didn't really elaborate. "Something like that. I would have to modify — as you put it."

Deep-rooted Celtic obstinacy moved in me. We'd spent the whole first part of the evening listening to this woman talk of herself: I wasn't about to be fobbed off. "You speak such beautiful English — you must have spent a whole lot of time there to acquire that accent — let alone your vocabulary." She sat at the end of the sofa where she had the fullest view from the plate glass window before the balcony. Jimmy had already preceded us with the demi-tasse cups and tall copper coffee-maker. She signalled no milk nor sugar as he poured for her, while addressing me again.

"Even in the war when I was not much more than a schoolgirl, I was constantly crosing the channel under the nose of the Germans. My mother was part-English, you see. And part-Russian. So I grew up really trilingual. Cambridge helped enormously of course. And Mother's family — they're a cadet line of the Portland's — well, while they were living we were very, very close, don't you know."

But my interest had been re-primed by her Russian allusion. There had been a time when I had seriously considered leaving Anglicanism and becoming Orthodox. I had actually lived in student digs in a large Baywater house run by a group of Russian Orthodox for university undergraduates with Russian interests. "Your grandmother was Rusian-born?" I enquired.

"My mother's father," she explained. "He was cousin to Prince Yousepoff — Rasputin's nemesis, don't you know."

That was the juncture, I think, when I began to build a slow burn. Her breezy 'don't you know' irritated on its own account, but it was the little lesson in Russian history which angered me more. Besides, it was all too pat. Somehow I couldn't just believe that all roads led directly to her. As if it wasn't enough to know that she had WW2 wrapped up, the Royal Family, Debrett, France, Academia and now Holy Russia (and probably the goddamn Revolution!) it seemed that there was no escape *whatever*. I experienced a kind of conversational paranoia — and it was in the expanding power of that, that I embarked on a course of mischief.

The beginnings seemed innocent enough. "I suppose your extended knowledge of the British Isles doesn't extend to Cornwall?"

"Your birthplace? Oh, indeed! When I was in Cheltenham — just for that year before I went up to Girton — Mummy and I spent a lot of the holidays at St. Michael's Mount with the St. Aubyns."

Damn her! "I meant the other end of the Duchy. Around Wadebridge? Port Isaac. I actually grew up in St. Kew. I doubt whether you've ever heard of that as there are no grand houses in the parish or even very much money."

"Of course I know it! It's between St. Minver to the south, St. Teath to the north, a bit of St. Endellion to the west I suppose and St. Maybyn to the east. Our friends Chula and Beira the Siamese chaps lived there. Beira was a motor racer but that was probably before your time."

"No," I said sullenly. Both leadenly aware of the identity of the two Siamese princes who had married British wives and of the total accuracy of her geographical knowledge of the region I knew best in the world. I tried another tack.

"In your London days, did you ever come across a character by the name of the Archimandrite Alexei Levertov?"

"Not in London," she said evenly. "But in Paris? He used to be a regular at the Bibliothèque Nationale although I understand he spent a lot of time in the B.M. too. How did *you* get to know the old man?"

"I met him in Paris first," I confessed reluctantly. "I forgot about that. Then I knew him at the British Museum — just like you said."

Connie had now rejoined us, picking up the threads of our conversation and tried to act as my ally in what obviously seemed to her a lop-sided state of affairs. "Why don't you ask Monique whom she *doesn't* know, Davey. That might prove more interesting."

But I had already decided on my course of action for I had just received an abrupt bolt of inspiration. "Would you by chance know some old friends of mine who spent quite a bit of wartime in France as liaison with the French Resistance and were actually deeply involved in counter-espionage for the British government. Name of Carr — Sir Sidney and Lady Carolyn? Although in those days he hadn't inherited the baronetcy and was just Colonel Carr, I imagine."

Monique looked flushed and her eyes glittered. I wondered how many Drambuies she had tossed back as we sat there, the sea and the stars a dark but perforated backdrop behind us. "That name rings a bell, by God it rings a bell! Tell me more."

I was only too eager to do so, now that my imagination was firmly in place. "Lady Carolyn was a Carlisle and I think someone told me that they had the controlling shares in the Rolls Royce company. Indeed, it was Colonel Carr's father who had started old Henry Rolls off in the first place. I saw a picture of Carolyn Carr in The Tatler when I was last in the Vancouver Club and she is still a beautiful woman."

"Of course I know them," said Monique, mercifully swallowing the bait. "The Carlisle couple! Yes, of course! My recollection of that daring pair is only scanty over their visit to our house in 1941 but when I was in India with my father in 1947 for the Independence Ceremonies by Lord Louis Mountbatten I have a vivid memory of your Sidney Carr holding up the honour of the dying Raj against a polo team composed of officers with the King's Own Ghurkha Rifles. And at the dinner that night in Delhi, Lady Carolyn gave a speech which many there described as being even wittier than any given by Lady Edwina Mountbatten herself."

I was beginning to enjoy myself. "My first memory is more prosaic. Were you ever at their place, Royal Liver, and did you ever encounter their brace of Borzois, Rolls and Royce?"

"The dogs escape me. But both with Daddy — who knew many of the Carrs when he was at the Court of St. James as a member of the French Embassy staff — and on my own — I have spent many a happy day at Royal Liver. Hampshire, wasn't it?"

"Liverpool," I corrected triumphantly. "And I don't think they were in India in '47 as they were busy mending dilapidated Rolls Royces."

Connie looked at me as if I'd gone crazy. "I thought you said they *owned Rolls Royce or had big shares in it.*"

"*I did. Anything to trap her* in her nonsense stories!"

If Connie looked as if I'd taken leave of my sense, Monique's expression suggested I was about to rape her. "I don't know what on earth you're talking about."

"I know you don't. That was my idea — precisely!"

Jimmy chose that moment to bounce back from his den with a finger stuck into a largish book. "Got it," he announced. "Extra strong peppermint at a Royal funeral when the embalming got screwed up."

"The pigeons are coming home to roost," Connie cooed. Even Robert, who when he wasn't doing his City Council routine tended to silence, now got into the act. "With all your connections I bet you've been in some pretty classy English gardens. Like Stourhead, Wilton and gems like Nymans."

"I know the Messells at Nymans — even if your friend here, finds it hard to believe. I won't mention the Armstrong-Jones connection and Princess Margaret or he'll cross-examine me again and try and trap me."

"You dig your own holes. You need no help from me," I said coldly.

"I was more interested in the fishpond and herbaceous border as I've done things along those lines here in Vancouver," said Robert, obviously anxious to restore harmony.

I wasn't through though. Indeed, as I felt my body stiffen with resolve there on the ample sofa, I knew I had hardly begun.

"If you know the Carrs — who live near Tatlow Park in Kitsilano, by the way, then I'm your grandfather. And if you've stayed at the Royal Liver then you've stayed in a large tower on the Liverpool waterfront owned by an insurance company. I doubt if old Sid Carr with his Lancashire accent has ever sat on a bloody horse, let alone a polo pony. But he knows a standard poodle when he sees one even if he might think the Court of St. James was a bloody police court. That's where you made your mistake, see. You people always let yourselves get carried away. Old Archimandrite Alexei you might well know — considering he was as oddball as yourself. And there's no reason you don't know Cornwall as well as the other million and a half tourists it sees each year.

Monique stood up. I was again made conscious of how small she was. "I refuse to stay here and be insulted by a bunch of uncouth yokels who refuse to accept one's word! What a boring lot you are! Not a scrap of intelligent conversation between you."

Connie glowered up at her. "No one else got a chance honey. You're into monologue, you know."

Monique's mouth could hardly have curled more in contempt. "From the moment I set eyes on you I expected nothing better than vulgar sniping or commonplace coment What I didn't know was that mediocrity moves here in packs. Your pedestrian minds are interchangeable! James, my coat please!"

She began to move towards the hallway and closet. The four of us, standing and sitting, exchanged glances uncertainly. Vancouver has no choreography for party-disintegration. By the time she reached the door and Jimmy had reached her side to help her on with her coat and hand her the tiny green umbrella she'd brought, the rest of us were bunched behind him. "I'm sorry," Jimmy began. "The embalming story didn't really matter."

Her now gloved hand waved all such protestation aside as she turned her back on our company and waited for the apartment door to be opened. "Not half as sorry as I am," she announced to the glossy cream wood. "The mistake was all mine, I assure you."

I found my voice again, only as she stepped across the hall to the elevator. "You don't have to do it, you know. Vancouver can be impressed by just the plain truth."

But that firm little neck so erectly supporting her trim black coiffeur, didn't turn by a centimeter. In fact I never saw Monique Marie Benoit again as she decided, so Jimmy subsequently informed us, that UBC wasn't her style after all and she resigned abruptly and surfaced a year later on the San Jose campus of the University of California. Of course, one has to remember that in those days, jobs were plentiful and it was a teachers' market.

MOSAIC PRESS FICTION SERIES

Quality fiction at reasonable prices

Fool by Leon Whiteson
The Gates by Marion Andre Czerniecki
A Long Way to Oregon by Anne Marriott
A Strange Attachment and Other Stories by Bibhutibhusan Bandyopadhyay,
　Translated from the Bengali by Phyllis Granoff
Cracked Wheat and Other Stories by Hugh Cook
A Dialogue with Masks by Mary Melfi
The Far Side of the River: Selected Short Stories by Jacob Zipper,
　Translated from the Yiddish by M. Butovsky
Big Bird in the Bush: Stories and Sketches by Earle Birney
The Honey Drum: Seven Tales from Arab Lands by Gwendolyn MacEwen
Summer at Lonely Beach and Other Stories by Miriam Waddington
The Suicide by Nikolai Erdman
　Translated from the Russian by A. Richardson & Eileen Thalenberg
Cogwheels and Other Stories by Akutagawa Ryunosuke
　Translated from the Japanese by E. Norman

Forthcoming:
Vibrations in Time by David Watmough
A Long Night of Death by Alberto Balcarze